year84

Brennan Conaway

———————

year84

Brennan Conaway

First edition September 2023
ISBN 979-8-218-23418-8

Publisher
Ministry of Truth

Writer
Brennan Conaway

Creative
Typesetting by Rion Echigo
Cover Design by Rion Echigo

Dedication
This book is dedicated to Etsuko and Shion

year84

Intro

It was a simple idea. Translate *Nineteen Eighty-Four* into Newspeak, the language George Orwell invented and introduced within that very same novel. I imagined it would be a metalinguistic ouroboros.

And it would be a first. I didn't know of any books written in Newspeak, which struck me as odd. Why hadn't anyone done this before? It should be easy: Unify all synonyms into one word (anything positive = *good*), add the prefix un- to make the antonym (*ungood*), and seed the text with *plus* and *doubleplus* for emphasis or exclamation. *The Principles of Newspeak*, in the book's appendix, seemed to be an instruction manual, but when it came to the nuts-and-bolts of grammar and lexical rules, I found some of the principles contradicted each other, and there were only three examples of short Newspeak sentences for guidance. I realized that Orwell presents Newspeak as a conceptual language, or maybe only as a concept about language.

Orwell seems to know that Newspeak is a mess. He reports that 'No etymological principle was followed' and 'words were not constructed on any etymological plan.' This humorous understatement (*Principles* that follow no principle) indicates that the masterminds at the Ministry of Truth are just a bunch of amateurs, which was a liberating revelation. If Orwell envisioned Newspeak as an ill-conceived plan implemented haphazardly, then I had some freedom in my own envisioning of the language. I didn't have to worry about making mistakes as I tried to discover what Newspeak looks like on the page, because the language itself is a mistaken attempt to reword English.

For help, I turned to Comrade Syme, the 'specialist in Newspeak' in *Nineteen Eighty-Four*, and listened to his idiotic rhapsodizing:

'It's a beautiful thing, the destruction of words.'

I went on a killing spree, hunting down synonyms, antonyms, redundancies, oldspeak, and unwords. I cut *Nineteen Eighty-Four* in half, from 104,000 words in Orwell's original to 52,000 words in *year84*. Along the way, I garbled the speech of the proletariats, reduced the vocabulary by eliminating single-use words, and dulled Orwell's subtlety and richness of expression. Continuing with the metaphor of the tail-eating snake (and the tale-eating snake), I limited the lexicon to those words, or their derivatives, which were already in the book, followed *The Principles* as best I could, and referred only to Orwell's writing to rewrite Orwell's writing. This translation process was a closed loop.

After making thousands of cuts, I had a Newspeak version of *Nineteen Eighty-Four*, but my work wasn't done. The story itself instructed me to be profoundly malicious. If I was going to act as a Ministry of Truth censor, I would have to produce an 'ideological translation.' Comrade Syme explains:

'By 2050...The whole literature of the past will have been destroyed...they'll exist only in Newspeak versions, not merely changed into something different, but actually changed into something contradictory of what they used to be.'

This meant changing *Nineteen Eighty-Four* in such a way that Orwell contradicts himself. The tragic story of Winston's attempt to rebel against a totalitarian government and celebrate his love for Julia becomes, through ideological translation, the triumphant tale of a brotherly bureaucracy returning a citizen to sanity after crimethink has put him in danger. Newspeak made this process of vilifying Winston much easier. When *sexcrime*, for example, is the only way to describe making love on a warm spring day, then Winston becomes a *criminal*, as defined in the Newspeak Dictionary.

As a censor at the Ministry of Truth, I forced myself to see Winston as mean-spirited and selfish, with a shameful backstory. As a boy he was vicious, repeatedly stealing food from his baby sister and eventually forcing his mother out of their home, causing the death of herself and her baby girl. As an adult, Winston married Katharine, but soon separated because he was too self-centered to love her or be intimate with her. At the beginning of *Nineteen Eighty-Four*, Winston is drinking gin for lunch and badmouthing Big Brother in his diary. As the novel progresses, he makes snide comments about nearly everyone. He thinks all children are brats. He's a misogynist who fantasizes about a sadistic rape-killing when he first meets Julia, buys sex from poor women in the proletarian district, and often has Oedipal dreams about his mother. He's too self-involved to be a good judge of character, so he mistakes friend for foe, foe for friend. His mentor O'Brien eventually intervenes and brings him back to sanity, after his crazy fling with Julia. At the end of *Nineteen Eighty-Four*, Winston is still drinking gin, alone in a crowded cafe, Big Brother his only friend.

This counter-narrative was helped along by more censorship: I referred to Winston by his government name, 6079 Smith, so that he would be less remarkable; removed references to England, to make the story placeless; altered dates, so it's timeless; redacted Winston's proof that the past has been altered; removed references to Eastasia and Eurasia, because it's a forever war; excised Goldstein's book as heretical; blanked out government violence and torture, so the Thought Police just ask people questions; exterminated all descriptions of rats; and emphasized the medical aspects of enhanced interrogation, to show O'Brien helping Winston regain his sanity.

I was also required to rewrite some of the stuff that I liked the best. The mocking absurdity of the Party slogans (War Is Peace, Freedom Is Slavery, Ignorance Is Strength) is the lens through which I view government propaganda and corporate happy-talk, but Comrade Syme knows what's coming:

'Even the slogans will change. How could you have a slogan like "freedom is slavery" when the concept of freedom has been abolished?'

I was just following orders when I rewrote them:

> Forever at War
> Joyful in Work
> Strong in Party

Throughout this complex process, which started with one simple idea, I've tried to remain true to *The Principles* and loyal to the Party, obey the internal logic of *Nineteen Eighty-Four*, and produce a translation that's doubleplus Orwellian.

Brennan Conaway
Kawasaki, Japan
April 2023

part01

chapter01

It was a lightful cold day in month04, and the clocks were flashing 13:00. 6079 Smith, his chin down in an attempt to avoid the plusungood wind, goed speedwise thru the glass doors of Winful House, tho underspeedwise to stop a spiral of dust from inning with him.

The hallway smelled of uncold stew and new carpets. A color poster, overbig for inside, was on the wall. It showed an oversize face, 1m broad: the face of a man about age45, with heavy black mustache and strongwise beautyful. Smith goed to the stairs. It was unuseful attempting the upper. It was sometimes unworking, and now the electric stream was knifed during daylight hours, saving and prepping for Unluv Week. His room was on level07, and Smith, who was age39 and had a dishealthful leg, upped unspeedwise, stopping a few times on the way. On every level, opposite the upper doors, the poster with the oversize face watched from the wall. The eyes followed him when he moved.

BB IS WATCHING YOU

Inside his room a speaker was reading a list of numbers about the production of metal. The speaking comed from the oval metal telescreen, nearsame an unclear mirror, on the right wall. Smith downed the sound, but the words stayed hearable. The telescreen was able to be downlighted, but there was noway to off it. He moved to the window: an unbig unpowerful man, his overthin body only highlighted by blue coveralls, the Party uniform. His hair was light-brown, his face red, his skin unsmoothed by unsmooth soap and unsharp razors and the cold of the ante-winter.

Outside, thru the unopened window, the world was cold. Down in the street unstrong wind was spiraling dust and paper, and tho the sun was up and the sky an unfull blue, everything was uncolorful, except the posters that were everywhere. The black-mustache face downwatched from every corner. There was 1 on the housefront opposite.

BB IS WATCHING YOU

The unlightful eyes deep-watched Smith's eyes. Down at street level another poster, ripped at 1 corner, moved on-and-off in the wind, covering and uncovering the words *The Party*. Plusunnear, a helicopter flyed between the roofs, stopped for a second nearsame a bug, and reflyed away: Thinkpol, watching persons thru windows.

Behind Smith the telescreen was loudspeaking about metal and the overfulled 3YP09. The telescreen broadcast 2-way sametimewise. Any sound that Smith maked, louder than pluslow unloudspeak, was heared by it, and if he stayed within its field, he was watched. There was noway of knowing when he was being watched. Which system, or what times, Thinkpol connected was unknowed. It was possible they watched everybody always. They were able to connect to his telescreen whenever they wanted to. He must act—did act, from habit that becomed animalthink—as if every sound he maked was overheared and, except in unlight, every move watched.

Smith had his back turned to the telescreen. It was safer; tho, as he knowed, even his back was unable to mask facecrime. 1km away, Minitrue, where he worked, towered plusbig and white over the unclean cityscape. This, he thinked with unclear unluv—this was the biggest city of Airfield01, Oceania. The Minitrue building was shockwise unsame anything else. An oversize pyramid of mirror-white concrete, flying up, levels-and-levels-and-levels, 300m into the air. From where Smith standed it was possible to read, on its whiteface in beautyful words, the 3 truewords of the Party:

FOREVER AT WAR
JOYFUL IN WORK
STRONG IN PARTY

Minitrue had 3,000 rooms overground and 3,000 rooms sublevel. In the city, 3 other white pyramids were nearsame oversize. So doubleplus did they unbig other buildings that from Winful House he was able to watch all of them sametimewise: Minitrue produced news and entertainment. Minipax: war. Miniluv: law and order. Miniplenty: money.

Miniluv was true terrorful. There were no windows in it. Smith had never been inside Miniluv or within .5km of it. It was unpossible to go, except on Party work, and then only by going thru a maze of razorwire, metal doors, and machineguns. Even the streets leading to its outer walls were watched by flatface safeguards in black uniforms, armed with rubber clubs.

Smith turned round speedwise. He had a face of unloud joy, which was goodest to wear when facing the telescreen. He crossed the room to the doubleplusunbig kitchen. By leaving Minitrue at this time of day he had unfeeded in the cafe, and he knowed there was no feed in the kitchen except bread, which he must save for post-day meal. From the shelf, he downed a bottle of uncolorful liquid: Winful Harddrink. It gived off an unhealthful oil-smell. Smith fulled a cup, nerved himself for a shock, and drinked it nearsame drugs.

Speedwise his face turned red and water outstreamed his eyes. The stuff was nearsame acid, nearsame being hitted on the head with a rubber club. But post-second, the fire in his belly downed and the world started to be joyfuller. He returned to the life-room and sitted at an unbig table to the left of the telescreen. He outdrawered a penholder, a bottle of ink, and an unthin midsize blank-book with a red cover.

The telescreen in the life-room was in an unusual position. Not placed, as usual, in the end wall, where it was able to watch the whole room, it was in the longer wall, opposite the window. To oneside of it there was a blank place, maybe for bookshelfs, in which Smith was now sitting. By sitting there, Smith stayed outside the telescreen field. He was able to be heared, but if he stayed in his present position he was unwatched. It was the unusual floorplan of the room that had helped him plan for what he was about to do.

But it had also been helped by the book that he had outdrawered. It was an unusual beautyful book. Its smooth white paper, yellowed by age, was a type unproduced for 40 ante-years. But he thinked the book was older than that. He had finded it in the window of a disorderful unbig freemarket in an unmoneyed district of the city and had been hitted speedwise by an overstrong want to deal it. Party members weren't OKed to deal on the freemarket, but Smith unfollowed the law. He had speedwise up- and downwatched the street and then unloudwise goed inside and dealed the blank-book. At the time he unwanted it for any reason. Shameful, he carried it to Winful House in his workcase. Even with nothing writed in it, it was a crimeful thing.

The thing that he was about to do was start a daybook. This wasn't outlawed (nothing was outlawed), but if watched, he would be stopped and questioned and work in joycamp for 25 post-years. Smith placed a pen into the penholder. Pens were overold, used only sometimes to sign, but he had dealed it, underhanded and difficult, because he feeled the beautyful smooth white paper needed to be writed with a pen, not scratched with an ink-pencil. He wasn't habitful in handwriting. Except plusunlong notes, it was usual to speakwrite everything, which was unpossible for this crimethink. He wetted the pen in the ink and then stopped for a second. His belly shaked. To write on the paper was the final act. In unbig crosswise words he writed:

day04 month04 year84

He stopped. A feeling of unpower downed him. To start with, he unknowed if this was year84. It was nearsame that date, because he thinked he was age39, and he thinked he was born in year44 or year45; but it was unpossible to know the date 100%.

For who, he speedwise thinked, was he writing this daybook? For the future, for the unborn. His mind flyed round the questionful date on the page, and then banged into doublethink. He now understanded the size of what he was undertaking. How was he able to speak to the future? It was unpossible. Either the future would be nearsame the present, so they would unhear him; or it would be unsame, and his problems would be unmeaningful.

For sometime he sitted, unthinkful, with the blank paper. The telescreen changed to loud military music. He had unpower to write and even disremembered what he had planned to write. For ante-weeks he had been prepping for this, and it had uncrossed his mind that anything was needed except heart. The writing would be undifficult. All he must do was place on the paper the unstopping ever-moving self-conversation that had been running inside his head for years. But now the self-conversation had stopped. And his leg was over-dishealthful. He unscratched it, because if he did it always becomed ungooder. The seconds were clicking away. He watched the blank page, feeled his dishealthful leg, heared the overloud music, and feeled unbigwise harddrinkful.

Speedwise he started writing in overterror, unknowing what he was writing. His unbig but over-youthful handwriting outspreaded up-down the page, dropping upper letters and even full stops:

day04 month04 year84. Ante-PM to the movies. All war movies. 1 plusgood of a boatful of outsiders being bombed somewhere in the south. Watchers plusenjoyed doubleplusbig unthin man attemptingto swim away with a helicopter gunning him, we watched him unspeedful-moving in the water nearsame a fish, then we watched him thru the helicopters guns, then he was full of holes and the ocean round him turned light-red and he downed speedwise as tho the holes had instreamed the water, watchers loudspeaking with joyspeak when he downed. then we watched a lifeboat full of youths with a helicopter overflying it. there was a mid-age woman sitting in the front with an unbig youth about age03 in her arms. unbig youth loudspeaking with terror and his head between her breasts as if he was attempting to hole into her and the woman with her arms round him and attempting to help him tho she was blue with terror herself, always covering him as if she thinked her arms were able to safeguard him from the bullets. then the helicopter dropped a 20kg bomb on them with terrorful flash and the boat goed all to pieces. doubleplusgood, a youth's arm going up-up up-up into the air and there was loudspeaking from the Party members but a woman down in the prole section of the movie-house speedwise started counter-loudspeaking they shouldnt of showed it not in front of youths they didnt it aint correct not in front of youths it aint thinkpol stopped her i unthink anything happened to her nobody cares what the proles speak about usual prole react they never...

Smith stopped writing, semi-because his hand muscles were overtight. He unknowed what had maked him outstream this waste. But the unusual thing was: while he was writing, a doubleplusunsame memory had become clear in his mind and he nearwise wanted to write it. It was, he now knowed, because of this other event that he had speedwise returned to Winful House and started the daybook today.

It had happened that AM at Minitrue, if he was able to speak about anything so shadowful as having *happened.*

It was nearwise 11:00, and in Recdep, where Smith worked, they were outpulling chairs from cubicles and grouping them mid-room, opposite the big telescreen, prepping for 2minUnluv. Smith was taking his place in a mid-row when 2 persons who he had watched, but had unspeaked to, comed into the room. 1 of them was a girl who he watched manytimes in the hallways. He unknowed her name, but he knowed that she worked in Ficdep. Maybe—he had sometimes watched her with oilful hands and carrying a wrench—she was a machineer on the book-writing machines. A strong heartful spirited girl with unthin blackhair, a light-brown face, and speedful sportful moves. A red waist-tie, sign of Youth Antisex League, was round the waist of her coveralls, tight enough to highlight the shape of her hips.

Smith unluved her because of the atmosphere of gamefields and cold baths and commwalks and clean-minds which she carryed with her. He unluved nearwise all womans, and doubleplusunluved the youthful and beautyful girls. Womans, youthful womans, were always serious Party followers, indrinkers of truewords, Party spys, and finders of ungoodthink. But he thinked this girl was plusunsafe. In the room, she speedwise sidewatched him, which arrowed into him and fulled him with black terror. It had even crossed his mind that she maybe a Thinkpol agent. He ever-feeled an unusual worry, a mix of terror and unluv, whenever she was anywhere near him.

The other person was a man named O'Brien, an Inner Party member with an important position, unlightful and unnear, that Smith unknowed. A speedful unsound overcomed the group round the chairs, as they watched the black coveralls of an Inner Party member coming. O'Brien was a big strong man with an unthin neck and an unsmooth, joyful, coldhearted face. Tho he was terrorful, he also had a joyful way. He had a trick of rewearing his eyeglasses which was unusualwise winning—in some unknowed way, civilized. It was a trick which showed he was true. Smith had watched O'Brien maybe 12 times in nearwise 12 years. He feeled deep-pulled to him, because he was interested in the unsame of O'Brien's gentle moves and his overpowerful body-type, and doubleplus because of an unwatched think—maybe not even a think, only a hope—that O'Brien ungoodthinked. Something in his face, but maybe it wasn't even ungoodthink writed in his face, but knowledge. Maybe he was a person to speak to, if Smith was able to avoid the telescreen and meet him single. Smith had unmaked the unbiggest attempt to verify it: there was noway of doing it.

O'Brien speedwise watched his clock—it was nearwise 11:00—and thinked to stay in Recdep for 2minUnluv. He taked a chair in the same row as Smith, a few places away. An unbig blondhair woman who worked in a cubicle near Smith was between them. The blackhair girl was sitting behind him.

The post-second, a doubleplusunbeautyful grinding sound, as of some overbig animal-machine running without oil, bursted from the big telescreen at the room-end. It was a sound that he feeled in his tooths and upped the hair on his neck. The Unluv had started.

As usual, the face of Goldstein, Enemy of the Party, flashed onscreen. There was unjoyspeak here-and-there. The unbig blondhair woman speaked with a mix of terror and disgust. Goldstein was an ex-leader of the Party, but had changed to counterRevolutioner. The 2minUnluv telecasts changed day-to-day, but Goldstein was always betrayer01. All antiParty crimes—all acts of workstop and betrays of goodthink—comed straight from his teaching. Somewhere he was starting his counterRevolution: maybe somewhere over the ocean, under the safeguard of outside powers, maybe even—it was sometimes storyed—in some unwatched-place in Oceania.

Smith's belly was tight. He was unable to watch Goldstein without an unjoyful mix of feelings. It was a thin face, with doubleplusbig whitehair—a thinkful face, but deep-within unluvful, oldthinkful, unserious. Long thin nose and eyeglasses, nearsame sheepface, and the speaking was also sheepful. Goldstein was loudspeaking anti-Orders of the Party—so overbig and doubleplusunusual that a schooler should be able to unthink it, but shockful possible that other persons, minusmindful, maybe cothinked it. Behind his head on the telescreen, enemy troops marched in long lines—rows-and-rows of solid mans with flatfaces, who comed to the screenfront and outwhited, replaced by others nearsame. The unsharp rhythm of the trooper boots backgrounded Goldstein's sheepspeak.

30 post-seconds from the Unluv start, uncontrollable loudspeaks of unjoy were outbreaking from half the persons in the room. The self-satisfyed sheepface onscreen, and the terrorful power of the enemy behind it, were overplus: Goldstein, or even thinking of him, auto-produced terror and unjoy. Tho Goldstein was unluved and doubleplusunluved by everybody, tho everyday and 1,000 times a day, on telescreens, in newspapers, in books, he was breaked and showed to be a waste-pile of thinking—his power never downed. Always new crimethinkers were waiting to be offtracked by him. Everyday, betrayers and workstoppers were unmasked by Thinkpol. He was the leader of a plusbig shadowful enemy, an underground of counterRevolutioners single-minded about overthrowing the Party: the Brotherhood. There were also unloudspeaked storys of a terrorful book collecting all ungoodthinks, of which Goldstein was the writer and which outspreaded shadowwise, here-and-there. It was an unnamed book. Persons referenced it, crimethinkful, as *the book*. But he knowed of those things only thru unclear storys. The Brotherhood and *the book* were subjects that Party members unspeaked about.

In minute02, the Unluv was out-of-control. Persons were jumping up-down in their places and doubleplusloudspeaking in an attempt to overpower the disenjoyful sheepspeak that comed from the screen. The unbig blondhair woman had turned red and her mouth was opening and unopening nearsame a landed fish. Even O'Brien's heavy face was red. He was sitting plusstraight in his chair, his powerful chest full and shaking, as tho he were withstanding hits from a club. The blackhair girl behind Smith had started loudspeaking 'Pig!

Pig! Pig!' and speedwise she upped the heavy Dictionary and throwed it at the screen. It hitted Goldstein's nose; the speaker ever-speaking.

Smith was loudspeaking with the others and kicking his chair powerfulwise. The terrorful thing about 2minUnluv wasn't that he must playact, but that it was unpossible to avoid joining in. Within 30 post-seconds, a mask was always unneeded. A doubleplusunbeautyful overjoy of terror, wanting to kill, to hammer faces, streamed thru the whole group, nearsame an electric stream. But the overjoy was an unshaped unordered feeling which changed, nearsame the bullets from a machinegun. Smith's unluv wasn't antiGoldstein, but antiBB, antiParty, and antiThinkpol; and at those times his heart goed out to the single ungoodthinker onscreen. But the post-second, he crimestopped and togethered with the persons round him, and all that was speaked about Goldstein was true. At those times his unwatched unluv of BB changed to luv, and BB towered up, an overpowerful unterrorful safeguard, standing nearsame a stonewall. Goldstein, tho single and unpowerful, with questions about his existence, was a crimeful otherworlder, able to break civilization with his powerful speaking.

It was even possible, at times, to change his unluv this way or that by a volunteerful act. Speedwise, with the type of power which he pulled his head away from the pillow in an ungooddream, Smith replaced his unluv, from the face onscreen to the blackhair girl behind him. Clear beautyful daydreams flashed thru his mind. He would hammer her unlifeful with a rubber club. He would tie her naked to a tree and gun her body full of arrows. He would rape her and knife her throat at climax. Now, gooder-and-gooder, he knowed *why* he plusunluved her. He plusunluved her because she was youthful and beautyful and antisexful, because he wanted to sexcrime with her, but would never do it, because round her sweet soft waist, which speaked to him: round me with your arm, was only the safeguarding red waist-tie, overstrong sign of goodsex.

The Unluv upped to its climax. Goldstein becomed true sheepspeaking, and for a second his face changed into a true sheep. Then the sheepface changed into the flatface of an enemy trooper, who was running, doubleplusbig and terrorful, machinegunning, and jumping out of the telescreen; some persons in the front row pushed back, terrorful. But in the same second, pulling a deep unexciteful outbreath from everybody, the unluvful enemy face uniced into the face of BB: black mustache, powerful, unexciteful, and so plusbig that it nearwise fulled the telescreen. Nobody heared what BB was speaking. Then the face of BB outwhited, and the truewords of the Party outstanded big and clear:

FOREVER AT WAR
JOYFUL IN WORK
STRONG IN PARTY

But the face of BB stayed for a few seconds onscreen, as tho it stayed on everybody's eyeballs. The unbig blondhair woman had throwed herself onto the chair in front of her. With a shaking lowspeak that sounded nearsame 'My Saver!' she upped her arms to the screen. Then she downed her face in her hands, speaking unloud to BB.

The crowd started a deep, unspeedful, rhythmful song of 'B-B!... B-B!'—over-and-over-and-over, plusunspeedwise, with a longtime between *B* letter01 and *B* letter02—a heavy lowspeakful sound, animalful, in the background he thinked he heared the march of naked foots and the banging of drums. For maybe 30 post-seconds they did it. A rhythm manytimes heared in times of overfeeling, a song to the highest mind of BB, an act of self-change, a groupthinkful overpowering of the mind with rhythm. Smith's belly growed cold. In 2minUnluv he was unable to stop codreaming with the crowd, but this subhuman songing of 'B-B!...B-B!' always fulled him with terror. He songed with the others: it was unpossible to do otherwise. To mask his feelings, to control his face, to do what everybody was doing, was habitful. But for a few seconds his eyes maybe betrayed him: facecrime. And it was then that the important thing happened—if, truewise, it did happen.

Speedwise he catched O'Brien's eye. O'Brien had standed, unweared his eyeglasses, and was rewearing them with his trickful move. But there was a millisecond when their eyes meeted, and Smith knowed—yes, he *knowed!*—that O'Brien was thinking the samething. A clear message. It was as tho their minds had opened and thinks were streaming thru their eyes. 'I'm with you,' O'Brien was speaking to him. 'I know what you're feeling. I know all about you, your unluv, your disgust. But don't worry, I'm on your side!' And then the flash of knowing goed, and O'Brien was flatface, same as everybody else.

That was all, and he unknowed if it had happened. Those type of events were never redone. But he stayed hopeful that others were enemys of the Party. Maybe the storys of a plusbig underground counterRevolution were true—maybe the Brotherhood truewise existed! It was unpossible, tho there were always stops and answers and executions, to know 100% that the Brotherhood was a story from the past. Somedays he thinked it, somedays un-. There was unevidence, only unbig things that maybe meaned anything or nothing: parts of overheared conversation, unbig words on toilet walls—onetime, even, when 2 persons meeted, an unbig hand-move, maybe a sign of recognizing. It was all unknowed: he maybe daydreamed everything. He had returned to his cubicle unrewatching O'Brien. The think of recontacting, following their speedful contact, uncrossed his mind. It was unthinkable and unsafe, even if he knowed how to do it. For 1 second, 2 seconds, they had exchanged an unclear speedful eye, and that was the story-end. But even that was a memoryful event in his single ownlife.

Smith self-energized and sitted straighter. He belched. The harddrink was upping from his belly. His eyes rewatched the page. He finded that while he sitted unpowerful, remembering, he had also been auto-writing. And it was unsame the overunbig, disorderful handwriting. His pen had moved, unspeedful and joyful, over the smooth paper, printing in big orderful words, over-and-over-and-over:

DOWN WITH BB DOWN WITH BB DOWN WITH
BB DOWN WITH BB DOWN WITH BB DOWN
WITH BB DOWN WITH BB DOWN WITH BB
DOWN WITH BB DOWN WITH BB DOWN WITH
BB DOWN WITH BB DOWN WITH BB DOWN
WITH BB DOWN WITH BB DOWN WITH BB
DOWN WITH BB DOWN WITH BB DOWN WITH
BB DOWN WITH BB DOWN WITH BB DOWN
WITH BB DOWN WITH BB DOWN WITH BB
DOWN WITH BB DOWN WITH BB DOWN WITH
BB DOWN WITH BB DOWN WITH BB DOWN
WITH BB DOWN WITH BB DOWN WITH BB
DOWN WITH BB DOWN WITH BB DOWN WITH
BB DOWN WITH BB DOWN WITH BB DOWN
WITH BB DOWN WITH BB DOWN WITH BB
DOWN WITH BB DOWN WITH BB DOWN WITH
BB DOWN WITH BB DOWN WITH BB DOWN
WITH BB DOWN WITH BB DOWN WITH BB
DOWN WITH BB DOWN WITH BB DOWN WITH
BB DOWN WITH BB

He was unable to stop the feeling of terror. It was unthinkful, because writing those words was the same crimethink as starting the daybook, but he thinked of ripping out the unclean pages and crimestopping.

He undid it, because he knowed it was unuseful. If he writed DOWN WITH BB, or if he crimestopped writing it, maked unchange. If he writed in the daybook, or if he unwrited in it, maked unchange. Thinkpol would stop him the sameway. He had done—even if he had never writed in the daybook—the crime that holds all others within itself: crimethink. Crimethink was unable to stay unwatched forever. He maybe sidestep for sometime, even for years, but unlater-or-later they were going to stop him.

It was always PM stops. The speedwise unsleep, the unsmooth hand shaking his shoulder, the overlights in eyes, the hardfaces round the bed. No trial, no report of the stop. Persons vaporized, always PM stops. Names were blanked from records, every record of everything cleaned up, onetime existence disremembered. He would be stopped, *vaporized*.

He was overtaked by unsane feelings. He started writing in speedful disorderful letters:

i dont care i dont care down with BB i dont care down with BB

He sitted in his chair, shameful, and downed the pen. Speedwise, he was shocked by knocking at the door.

So speedful! He sitted unmoving, with the unuseful hope that the person would go away. But no, there was reknocking. The ungoodest thing was an unspeedful answer. His heart was drumming, but his face, from longtime habit, was flatface. He upped and moved, unspeedful, to the door.

chapter02

As he placed his hand on the door, Smith watched that he had leaved the daybook open on the table. DOWN WITH BB was writed allover it, in words nearwise big enough to be readable from the doorway. It was an unthinkful thing to have done. But, he knowed, even in his terror he unwanted to unclean the smooth white paper by unopening the book while the ink was wet.

He inbreathed and opened the door. Speedwise, uncold unexcite streamed thru him. An uncolorful woman, with thin hair and lined face, was standing outside.

'O, Smith,' she downspeaked in an unlifeful way, 'I thinked I heared you come in. Do you think you're able to come over and repair our kitchen sink? It's stopped and...'

It was Parsons, the spouse of a coworker. She was a woman about age30, but her face was plusolder. He thinked there maybe dust in the lines of her face. Smith followed her down the hallway. These volunteer repairs were nearwise everyday duty. Winful House was an old building from year30, and Party members helped to repair the ceilings and walls, the tubes and the roof, and the windows. The AC system was usualwise at half-power for block savings. Committee members overwatched the building repairs.

'It's only because Tom isn't here,' speaked Parsons unclearwise.

The Parsons's life-room was bigger than Smith's, and unclean in an unsameway. Everything was disorderful and walked-on, as tho the place had been hitted by some big powerful animal. Sports stuff—balls, games, arrows, sweatpants turned inside-out—lay allover the floor, and the table was piled with unclean bowls, spoons, and old physed books. On the walls were red flags of Youth League and Spys, and a full-size poster of BB. There was the usual, everywhere smell of uncold stew and of a person who wasn't there now. In another room somebody with a toy trumpet was attempting to coplay the military music on the telescreen.

'It's my youths,' speaked Parsons, speedwise watching the door, half-worryful. 'They haven't goed out today. And...'

She had a habit of breaking off her sentences in the mid. The kitchen sink was full nearwise to the top with plusunclean greenwater, which malsmelled. Smith downed and watched the angle-connection of the tube. He unluved handwork, and he unluved downing with an unstraight back, which usualwise started him coughing. Parsons watched, unpowerful.

'If Tom was here he'd repair it speedwise,' she speaked. 'He's good with repairs. He's evergood with his hands, Tom is.'

'Tom'—Comrade Parsons—was Smith's coworker at Minitrue. Parsons was an unthin but sportful man, unthinking but goodthinking—one of those doubleplusunquestioning goodthinkers who, plus than Thinkpol, supported the Party. He had overstayed in Spys by 1 year, and had been outed from Youth League at age35. At Minitrue he worked in a sub-position which needed plusgoodthink, and he was a leader on Sportscom and other volunteer committees for organizing commwalks, unplanned demos, and savings plans. He speaked to Smith with unloud pride about being at every CommcenPM for 4 ante-years. But an overpowerful feeling of ungood, a type of unknowing about his own underlife, followed Parsons wherever he goed, and even stayed post-going.

'Do you have a wrench?' Smith questioned, playful working with the angle-connection.

'A wrench,' Parsons speedwise becomed gelful. 'I don't know... maybe my youths...'

There was a sound of boots and another blast on the trumpet as the youths banged into the life-room. Parsons bringed the wrench. Smith unfulled the sink and outpulled the disgustful hairball that had stopped the tube. He cleaned his fingers in cold water and returned to the other room.

'Up with your hands!' loudspeaked the youthful animal.

A beautyful, strong youth of age09 jumped from behind the table and threatened him with a toy machinegun, while his unbig sister, about age07, maked the same move with a piece of wood. Both of them weared blue pants, white shirts, and red neckties: the uniform of Spys. Smith upped his hands overhead, but he was worryful. The youth was overserious and coldhearted; it wasn't 100% a game.

'You're a betrayer!' loudspeaked the youth. 'You're a crimethinker! You're an enemy! I'll gun you, I'll vaporize you, I'll send you to the coal mines!'

Speedwise they were both jumping round him, loudspeaking 'Betrayer!' and 'Crimethinker!' the unbig girl copying her big brother in every move. It was unbig terrorful, nearsame the play of animals which will grow into killers. There was cold power in the youth's eye, a plusclear want to hit or kick Smith and self-knowing he was nearwise big enough to do so. It was good that it wasn't a true machinegun he was holding, Smith thinked.

Parsons's eyes moved, speedwise and worryed, from Smith to the youths, and rewatched Smith. In the gooder light of the life-room, he watched with interest that truewise dust was in the lines of her face.

'They get plusloud,' she speaked. 'They're disheartened because they're unable to watch the execution, that's what it is. I'm overworked, and Tom is working overtime.'

'Why're we unable to go and watch the execution?!' the youth doubleplusloudspeaked.

'Want to watch the execution! Want to watch the execution!' songed the unbig girl, jumping round.

Some POWs—warcrimers—were being executed in the park, Smith remembered. This happened everymonth, and was popular entertainment. Youths always loudspeaked to be taked to watch it. He goodbyed Parsons and outed the door. In the hallway, something hitted the back of his neck, as tho red fire had arrowed into him. He spiraled round ontime to watch Parsons pulling her youth inside, while he inpocketed the toy gun.

'Goldstein!' loudspeaked the youth as the door unopened on him. The woman's gray face was unpowerful, terrorful.

In his own room, he stepped speedwise past the telescreen and resitted at the table, touching his neck. The telescreen music had stopped, and a speedful militaryspeaker was reading, with a coldhearted joy, the stats of the new FF guns and rocket bombs.

With those youths, he thought, that unjoyful woman had a terrorful life. In a few years they would be watching her AM-PM for signs of ungoodthink. Nearwise all youths were dutyful. Organizations, nearsame Spys, systemwise changed them into unbig Party members, with Party habits. They luved the Party and everything connected with it. The songs, the parades, the flags, the commwalks, the machineguns, the loudspeaking of truewords, the worship of BB—it was a plusbeautyful game to them. All their power was outturned, antienemys of the Party, antioutsiders, antibetrayers, antiworkstoppers, anticrimethinkers. Persons plus age30 were terrorful of their youths. Everyweek *The Times* had a story of a youth hero who overheared some crimeful words and informed on their parents to Thinkpol.

The sharp unjoy of the toy bullet had stopped. He reupped his pen, halfhearted, thinking if he was able to find anything to write in the daybook. Speedwise he started rethinking of O'Brien.

He had dreamed 7 ante-years that he was walking thru a doubleplusblack room. And somebody sitting on the side speaked: 'We'll meet in the place where there's no unlight.' It was speaked plusunloud, nearwise unserious—a speak, not an order. He walked on, unstopping. In the dream, the words had been unimportant to him. But later, and unspeedful, they becomed important. Now he disremembered if time01 to watch O'Brien was ante- or post-dream, and he was unable to remember when he had IDed the dream speaker as O'Brien, but it was O'Brien who had speaked to him out of the unlight 7 ante-years.

Smith was unable to know—unpossible to know 100%—if O'Brien was an enemy or an unenemy. But it was unimportant. There was a connection of understanding between them, importanter than feelings or Party. 'We'll meet in the place where there's no unlight,' he had speaked. Smith unknowed what it meaned, but someway it would come true.

The telescreen stopped speaking. A trumpet call, clear and beautyful, streamed into the unmoving air. The telescreen reloudspeaked, ungentle:

'Attention! Your attention! A newsflash from the front: Our troops have a plusbeautyful win. We're now reporting the war maybe near its end. Here's the newsflash...'

Ungoodnews coming, thought Smith: a terrorful story about vaporizing the enemy, with doubleplusbig numbers of KIAs and POWs, and an update that, post-week, chocolate would be uprationed to 20g.

Smith rebelched. The harddrink had goed, leaving an unfull, unjoyful feeling. The telescreen—because of the win—started *Oceania, It's for You*. It was Party duty to stand at attention for the song, but he was unwatched, so he unstanded.

Oceania, It's for You changed to joyfuller music. Smith walked to the window, with his back to the telescreen. The day was cold and clear. Somewhere unnear a rocket bomb hitted with an unsharp, resounding blast. About 20 or 30 of them were dropping on the city everyweek.

Down in the street the wind moved the poster, and he watched, then unwatched: *The Party*. The Orders of the Party, doublethink, the changeable past. He felt he was walking at the bottom of the ocean, offtrack in an animal world where he was the animal. He was ownlife. The past was unlife, the future was unthinkable. How did he know that anybody, now, was on his side? That the Party wouldn't have power and control *forever*? As an answer to his questions, the truewords on the whiteface of Minitrue returned to him:

FOREVER AT WAR
JOYFUL IN WORK
STRONG IN PARTY

He outpocketed a coin. There, also, in doubleplusunbig clear words, the same truewords were writed, and on the otherside: BB. Even from the coin, the eyes watched him. On coins, on bookcovers, on flags, and on posters—everywhere. The eyes ever-watching him and the telescreens ever-speaking. Sleep or unsleep, working or feeding, inside or outside, in the bath or in bed—no out. Nothing was his ownlife except the few cubic cm inside his skull.

The sun had moved round, and the many windows of Minitrue, the sunlight not on them, were as unlightful serious as the eyes of a watchful safeguard. His heart shaked with terror in front of the oversize pyramid. It was overstrong, it was unable to be overcome. 1,000 rocket bombs wouldn't downhammer it. He rethinked for who he was writing the daybook. For the future, for the past—for a time that maybe a dream. And in front of him there layed not unlife but vaporization. The daybook would be fired to dust and he to vapor. Only Thinkpol would read what he writed, then they would unwrite it and blank it from memory. How was he able to speak to the future when none of him, not even a word writed on a piece of paper, was everlifeful?

The telescreen flashed 14:00. He must leave 10 post-minutes and return to work by 14:30.

Unusualwise, the flashing of the time uphearted him. He was an ownlife shadow speaking true. Nobody would hear him. But if he speaked it, in some unknowed way, the ever-true was unbreaked. He was unheared, but by staying sane, he stayed human. He returned to the table, holded his pen, and writed:

> To the future or the past, to a thinkful time, when persons are unsame and unsingle—to a true time when what is done isn't undone: From the time of same, from the time of single, from the time of BB, from the time of doublethink—hello!

He was unlifeful, he thinked. It was only now, when he had started to outwrite his thinks, that he had taked the final step. The end of every act is within the start of the act itself. He writed:

> Unlife is not part of crimethink: Crimethink IS unlife.

Now that he knowed he was an unlifeful man, it becomed important to hold life as longtime as possible. The fingers of his righthand were unclean with ink. It maybe unmasked him as an ownlifer. Some watchful goodthinker in Minitrue (somebody nearsame the blackhair girl from Ficdep) maybe start thinking why he had been writing during mealtime, why he had used an old pen, *what* he had been writing—and then inform the Party. He goed to the bathroom and carefulwise cleaned his hands with brown soap, which was nearsame sandpaper and good for this type of cleaning.

He indrawered the daybook. It was plusunuseful to think of making it unwatched, but he was able to know if Thinkpol had finded it. A hair on the page-ends was overclear. With his fingerend he upped a piece of white dust and placed it on the bookcover corner, where it would be shaked off, if the book was moved.

chapter03

Smith was dreaming of his parent. He was age10 or age11, he thinked, when she had been vaporized. She was a tall, beautyful, unspeakful woman with brownhair and unspeedful moves. She had been in the doubleplusbig cleanups of the year50s.

In Smith's dream, she was sitting someplace deep under him, with his youthful sister in her arms. He unremembered his sister, except as a doubleplusunbig, unstrong baby, always unspeakful, with big, watchful eyes. Both of them were upwatching him. They were down in some sublevel place—the bottom of a plusdeep hole—but it was a place which, now down, was moving downer. They were in a downing boat, upwatching him thru the unlightening water. There was air in the boat, they were able to watch him and he them, but they were downing, down-down, into the greenwater which in another second would have them forever. He was out in the light and air while they were being pulled down to unlife, and they were down there *because* he was up here. He knowed it and they knowed it, and he was able to watch the knowledge in their faces. There was no unjoy in their faces or in their hearts, only the knowledge that they must unlife so he was able to have life, and this was part of the unavoidable order of things.

He disremembered what had happened, but he knowed in his dream that someway the lifes of his parent and his sister had been dealed for his ownlife. It was 1 of those dreams which was part of his mindful life: a post-sleep knowing of trues and thinks which are new and important. The thing that now speedwise hitted Smith was that his parent's unlife, 30 ante-years, had been unjoyful, and unjoyful in a way that was now unpossible. Unjoy, he knowed, was only in the doubleplusoldtime—the deep past—a time when there was ownlife, and persons standed together, unreasonful.

The memory ripped at his heart because he had been overyouthful and -ownlifeful. Those things, he knowed, unhappened today. Today there was terror and unluv, but not deep or complex unjoy. All this he watched in the big eyes of his parent and his sister, upwatching him thru greenwater, 100m down and ever-downing.

Speedwise he was standing on unlong soft grass, on a summer PM when the angling sunlight golded the ground. Smith rewatched this landscape manytimes in his dreams, and he unknowed if he had also truewise watched it. In his unsleeping thinks he called it Gold Country. It was an old field, with a foot-track going here-and-there. In the bushs on the opposite field-edge, the trees were moving plusunbigwise in the wind, their leafs moving nearsame woman hair. Somewhere near but unwatched, there was a clear, unspeedful stream where fish were swimming in the water under the trees.

The blackhair girl was coming to him thru the field. With a single move, she unweared her coveralls, prideful, and side-throwed them. Her body was white and smooth, but it upped unsexcrimethink in him. In that second, he overfeeled luv for the way she side-throwed her coveralls. Smooth and uncareful, it vaporized the whole society, the whole system, as tho BB and the Party and Thinkpol would all be nothing, by a single doubleplusgood arm-move. That also was a move from the doubleplusoldtime—the deep past. Smith unsleeped, underspeaking the word *Juliet*.

The telescreen blasted an overloud trumpet for 30 seconds. It was 7:15, getting-up time for office workers. Smith pulled his body out of bed—naked—and weared an unclean undershirt and sweatpants. Physed would start in 3 post-minutes. He doubled over with a powerful coughing, which always hit him post-sleep. It unfulled his lungs, and he was able to start rebreathing only by laying on his back and taking a series of deep inbreaths. The coughing had ungooded his dishealthful leg.

'Age30 to age40 group!' loudspeaked a sharpspeakful woman. 'Age30 to -40 group! Take your places. 30s to 40s!'

Smith jumped to attention in front of the telescreen and watched a youthful woman, thin but strong, in physed wear.

'Arms unstraightening and pushing!' she outspeaked. 'Take your time by me. 1, 2, 3, 4! 1, 2, 3, 4! Come on, with some life in it! 1, 2, 3, 4! 1, 2, 3, 4...'

The unjoy of the coughing hadn't 100% blanked the dream from Smith's mind, and the rhythmful moves of physed reminded him. As he machinewise moved his arms, wearing flat joyface, which was correct during physed, he was self-warring to remember the unlightful time of his youth.

It was doubleplusdifficult. Ante-year50s everything outwhited. There were unrecords that he was able to reference; the outline of his ownlife was unsharp. He remembered doubleplusbig events which maybe had unhappened, he remembered some events but not their atmosphere, and there were longtime blanks of nothing. Everything had been unsame then—the names of places and their shapes on the map—but Airfield01, he thought, had always been called Airfield01.

Smith disremembered a time when Oceania had not been at war. 1 of his youthful memorys was of an airwar which shocked everybody. Maybe it was the time they dropped the newtype bombs. He disremembered the war itself, but he remembered his parent's hand holding his own, as they speeded down-down-down to someplace deep sublevel, round-and-round the spiral stairs, which unstronged his legs and he started unjoyspeaking. His parent, in her unspeedful, dreamful way, was carrying his baby sister—maybe—he unknowed if his sister had been born then. Final they had come to a loud, crowded Tube station. There were persons sitting allover the stone floor, and other persons, overcrowded, were sitting on metal beds. Smith and his parent finded a place on the floor.

Post-years of that memory, war had been forever, but it hadn't always been the same war. For a few months during his youth there had been war in the city streets, which he remembered clearwise. But to know the whole history, to speak about who was warring who on anyday, was unpossible, because there was unwrited records and unspeaked words. Now, in year84, Oceania was at war with the enemy. It was never speaked that Oceania had at anytime been unwarring, but Smith thinked Oceania had been at war for only 4 ante-years. But that was only a piece of underhanded knowledge which he had because his memory wasn't undercontrol.

The terrorful thing—he everthinked, as he powered his shoulders back with hands on his hips (They were spiraling their bodies from the waist, good physed for the back muscles)—the terrorful thing was that it maybe all true.

The Party speaked that Oceania had forever been at war. He, 6079 Smith, thinked that Oceania was unwarring 4 ante-years. But where did that knowledge exist? Only in his own mind, which must later be vaporized. And if all others OKed that untrue—if all records were the same—then untrue becomed history and becomed true. 'Who controls the past,' speaked the Party trueword, 'controls the future: who controls the present controls the past.' If the past was rectifyable, it never had been rectifyed. Whatever was true now was true always and forever. It was plusundifficult. He needed a series of wins over his own memory: he needed to doublethink.

'Stand down!' loudspeaked the leader, plusjoyful.

Smith downed his arms to his sides and unspeedwise refulled his lungs with air. His mind dropped into the maze-world of doublethink. To know and unknow, to 100% know the true while speaking careful-builded untrues, to sametimewise contrathink and know of contrathinking, to feel uncorrect but speak correct (to think that safeguarding everybody was unpossible and the Party was the safeguard of everybody) to disremember whatever was unneeded, then repull it from memory when it was needed, and then speedwise redisremember it: and overall, to use the same process on the process itself. That was the final sharpthinking: thinkfulwise to be unthinkful, and then reunthinkful of doublethink. To understand the word *doublethink* Smith needed to use doublethink.

The leader called them to attention. 'And now watch! Which of us is able to touch our toes? Over from the hips. 1, 2! 1, 2!...'

Smith unluved this physed, which flashed unjoy allway up his legs and manytimes caused coughing. The half-joy outed his mind. The past, he thinked, hadn't only been rectifyed, it had been vaporized. How was he able to know even the clearest true, when records unexisted outside his own memory? He attempted to remember time01 when he had heared of BB. He thinked it was sometime in the year60s, but it was unpossible to know. In the Party history, BB was the leader and safeguard of the Revolution from day01. His heroful acts had been unspeedwise pushed back into the shadowful world of the year40s and -30s, when the freemarketeers in their unusual tophats moved thru the city streets. It was unknowed if this history was true or invented.

Smith disremembered when the Party had come into existence. He unthinked he had heared of the Party ante-year60, but it was possible that it had been ante-year60. Everything was shadows and vapor. It was writed in the Party history books that the Party had invented airplanes, but he remembered airplanes in his youth. He was able to evidence nothing. There was never any evidence...

'Smith!' loudspeaked the overstrong woman on the telescreen. '6079 Smith! Yes, *you*! Down, unstraighten! You're able to do gooder than that. You're not even attempting it. Down! *That's* gooder. Now, the whole squad, watch me.'

A terrorful plusuncold sweat was allover Smith's body. He stayed doubleplusflatface. Never disheartened! Never dissatisfyed! A single flash of the eyes maybe facecrime. He standed watching while the leader upped her arms overhead and—not smoothwise, but plusgood organized and ordered—unstraightened down, her fingers under her toes.

'*There*! That's how you do it. Rewatch me. I'm age39, and I'm a parent to 4 youths. Now watch.' She reunstraightened down. '*My* knees are straight. You're able to do it if you want to,' she speaked as she straightened herself up. 'Anybody under age45 is 100% able to touch their toes. We're unable to be on the frontline, but we're able to be healthful. Remember our troops on the frontlines! And the FF troops! Think of *them*. Now, reattempt. That's gooder, that's *plus*gooder,' she speaked, heartenful, as Smith, with a powerful downmove, touched his toes with knees straight: time01 in ante-years.

chapter04

With the deep, unthinkful outbreath which the near telescreen was unable to crimestop him from making at workstart, Smith pulled the speakwrite to him, undusted the mouthpiece, and weared his eyeglasses. Then he unrolled and paperclipped the 4 unbig tubes of paper which had dropped out of the newtube to the right of his desk.

In the walls of his cubicle there were 3 holes. To the right of the speakwrite, an unbig newtube for messages; to the left, a bigger newtube for newspapers; and in the sidewall, near Smith's arm, a big oval slit—a memory-hole—for wastepaper, safeguarded by a wire cover. Nearsame slits existed thruout the building, in every room and every hallway, for vaporizing any doc or paper. It was an auto-move to up the cover of the nearest memory-hole and drop in a piece of wastepaper, where it would spiral away on a stream of uncold air to the oversize fires in the sublevels of the building.

Smith readed the 4 pieces of paper which he had unrolled. Each holded a message of only 1 or 2 lines, in Minitrue workspeak:

times 17.03.84 bb speak malreported rectify
times 19.12.83 forecasts 3yp quarter04 83 misprints verify
times 14.02.84 miniplenty malquoted chocolate rectify
times 03.12.83 reporting bb dayorder doubleplusungood refs
        unpersons rewrite fullwise upsub anterec

With an unbig satisfyful feeling Smith sidelined message number04. It was complex and dutyful work, and he wanted it to be his final workpiece. The others were usual work messages; number02 would mean some overlong reading thru number lists.

Smith clicked *ante-numbers* on the telescreen for those numbers of *The Times*, which outed the newtube in only a few minutes. The messages referenced reports or news storys which for some reason needed to be rectifyed. For example, in *The Times* of day17 month03, BB had forecasted, in his ante-day Order for the Day, that the frontline would stay unwarful. BB's speak needed to be truewise rewrited. *The Times* of day19 month12 had published the Party production forecasts of consumer goods in quarter04, year83, which was also quarter06, 3YP09. Today's *Times* had a speak of the true production. Smith's work was to verify the numbers. Message number03 referenced an undifficult correct which he was able to rectify in a few minutes: in month02, Miniplenty had reported a chocolate downration maybe needed sometime in month04 year84. Over the weekend, as Smith knowed, the ration would up to 20g.

Smith verifyed the messages, paperclipped his speakwrited corrects to *The Times* copy, and inned them newtube. Then, with an auto-move which was nearwise unthinkful, he folded the message and any notes that he had maked, and memory-holed them, to feed the fire.

In the unwatched maze of newtubes, when all the corrects for a number of *The Times* were together and in order, that number was reprinted, the copy vaporized, and the correct copy placed in the records. This ever-rectifying process was used on newspapers, books, mags, booklets, posters, movies, soundtracks, photos—every media or doc which maybe important, of Party, or goodthinkful. Day-by-day and minute-by-minute, the past was updated. All history was an overwrited doc: razored clean and rewrited manytimes. The biggest section of Recdep was a squad whose duty was to trackdown and replace copys of books, newspapers, and other docs which were unrectifyed. A number of *The Times* which maybe rewrited manytimes was in the records, and another copy unexisted to opposite it. Books, also, were collected and rewrited and doublerewrited and republished. The Recdep messages always referenced miswrites, misprints, or malquotes which needed to be rectifyed and corrected.

Smith touched his nose gentlewise with a paperclip and watched Tillotson in his cubicle on the otherside of the hallway. He was an unbig careful man working, unchangeful, with a folded newspaper on his knee and his mouth plusnear the mouthpiece of the speakwrite, to stay unwatched what he was speaking to the telescreen. He upwatched, and his eyeglasses arrowed an unluvful flash at Smith.

Smith unfullwise knowed Tillotson or what he was working on. Persons in Recdep unspeaked about their work. In the long unwindowful room, with its double row of cubicles and the ever-sound of papers moving and workers speakwriting, there were many unnamed persons who Smith watched everyday, speeding here-and-there in the hallways or overmoving in 2minUnluv. In a near cubicle, the unbig woman with blondhair worked, day-in day-out, tracking down and rectifying the names of unpersons. Her work was blackwhiteful correct, as her spouse had been vaporized a few ante-years. And a few cubicles away an unstrong dreamful man named Ampleforth, plusgood at versifying songs and poems, was reproducing poems which had become ungoodthinkful.

This room, with its 50 workers, was only a subsection in the doubleplusbig Recdep complex. Under, over, everywhere—crowds of persons multiworked. Doubleplusbig printers, with subwriters, reworders, and photo rectifyers; Teledep with machineers, producers, and teams of playacters who copyed persons; reference workers listed books, newspapers, and mags to be collected; plusbig record-rooms of corrected docs; and fires where the copys were vaporized. And somewhere, unwatched and unknowed, the ordering brains planned and knowed the lines: which pieces of the past must stay, which must be rectifyed, or which must be vaporized.

And Recdep was only a single branch of Minitrue, whose importantest work was to supply Oceania with newspapers, movies, schoolbooks, telecasts, playacts, books—all info, media, or entertainment—statues, truewords, poems, thinkful writings, youth books, the Dictionary. Minitrue supplyed the multineeds of the Party and the proles, in the Prolefeed subsection.

Prolefeed produced books, music, movies; entertainment about sports, crimes and star signs; overshockful books, oversexful movies, and overfeelful songs which were machine-writed on an unusual kaleidoscope: a versifyer. And Pornosec produced the lowest porn, which was sended out in packs and which Party members were unOKed to watch.

A few messages had outed the newtube while Smith was working, but they were undifficult workpieces, and he did them ante-2minUnluv. When the Unluv ended, he returned to his cubicle, taked the Dictionary from the bookshelf, sidelined the speakwrite, cleaned his eyeglasses, and started his big AM workpiece.

Smith was joyful in work. It was ever-usual and overlong, but some workpieces were difficult and complex, and he was able to travel within them, as in a deep math problem—nothing to help him, except his knowledge of Orders of the Party and his thinking about what BB wanted. Smith was good at rewriting. Sometimes he even rectifyed *The Times* leading reports. He unrolled the message he had sidelined:

times 03.12.83 reporting bb dayorder doubleplusungood refs
unpersons rewrite fullwise upsub anterec

Smith touched his nose gentlewise with his eyeglasses, daydreaming. Speedwise there jumped into his mind, pre-prepped, the picture of Comrade Ogilvy, who was KIA, a hero. Sometimes BB used his Order for the Day to remember some dutyful Outer Party member whose life and unlife was an example to be followed. Today BB would remember Comrade Ogilvy. A few lines of print and a few rectifyed photos would bring him to life.

Smith thought for a second, then started speakwriting in BB's style: a style both militaryful and teacherful, questioning and then speedwise self-answering. It was undifficult to write.

At age03 Comrade Ogilvy unplayed with toys except a drum, machinegun, and helicopter. At age06—1 ante-year usual members—he joined Spys. At age09 he was a troop leader. At age11 he informed on his parent to Thinkpol post-overhearing a crimeful conversation. At age17 he was district organizer of Youth Antisex League. At age19 he maked a bomb for Minipax which, at use01, killed 31 POWs in 1 burst. At age23 he was KIA. Tracked down by enemy planes while flying over the ocean with important messages, he weighed down his body with his machinegun and jumped out of the helicopter into deep water, messages and all—an end, speaked BB, which was unpossible to think about unprideful. BB plussed a few words on Comrade Ogilvy's single-minded pure life. He was an antisexer and nondrinker, no rec except an hour everyday of physed, and taked a pledge of antisex, thinking marry was antiduty, 24/7, to Party. He had no subjects of conversation except Orders of the Party, and no life except overpowering the enemy and tracking-down betrayers, workstoppers, crimethinkers.

He speedwise rewatched his coworker in the opposite cubicle and thought Tillotson was overworking on the same story. It was unknowed whose workpiece would be used, but he feeled, plusdeep, that it would be his.

chapter05

In the low-ceiling cafe, deep sublevel, the meal line moved unspeedwise. The room was full and doubleplusloud. From the kitchen, the stew vapor outstreamed. On the otherside of the room, there was a hole in the wall, where harddrink was dealed at 10¢ for a big cup.

'The man I was watching for,' speaked somebody behind Smith.

He turned round. It was his coworker Syme, who worked in Resdep. Syme was a reworder on the doubleplusbig team writing Dictionary number11. He was a doubleplusunbig man, unbigger than Smith, with brownhair and big outful eyes, both unjoyful and counter-joyspeakful, that watched Smith's face carefulwise while they conversed.

'I wanted to question you, if you have any razors.'

'None!' speaked Smith with shameful speed. 'I've attempted allover the place. They unexist.'

Truewise, he had 2 unused razors, ownlifeful. He had dealed them, underhanded, on the freemarket.

'I've been using the same razor for 6 weeks,' he plussed, untrue.

The line restarted and stopped; he turned and refaced Syme. Each of them taked a clean metal tray from the pile.

'Did you go and watch the prisoners executed ante-day?' questioned Syme.

'I was working,' answered Smith, unfeelful. 'I'll watch it at the movies, I think.'

'Minusreplaceful.'

His counter-joyspeakful eyes moved over Smith's face. 'I know you,' the eyes speaked, 'I watch you. I plusknow why you ungoed to watch those prisoners executed.' In a mindful way, Syme was doublestrong goodthinkful. He speaked with unluvful satisfyful joy of helicopters blasting enemy citys, trials of crimethinkers, executions in the sublevels of Miniluv. When speaking to him, Smith ever-changed the subject to the stats of rewording the Dictionary, on which he was knowing and interesting. Smith turned his head to avoid the big watchful eyes.

'It was a good execution,' speaked Syme, remembering. 'I think it's ungood when they tie their foots. I enjoy watching them kicking and, at the end, the tongue out and blue—a pluslightful blue. That's the thing that speaks to me.'

'Nex'!' loudspeaked the kitchen worker in whitewear.

Smith and Syme pushed ahead their trays for their meals: a bowl of stew, bread and cheese, a cup of coffee, and a sugar tablet.

'There's a table over there, under that telescreen,' speaked Syme. 'Let's deal some harddrink on the way.'

The harddrink was served in unhandleful cups. They moved thru the crowded room and unpacked their trays onto the metal table. Smith upped his cup of harddrink, stopped for a second to nerve up, and drinked it. He outed tears from his eyes, and speedwise finded that he was hungerful. He started feeding, spoonfuls of stew and meat cubes. They unrespeaked until they had unfulled their bowls. From the table at Smith's left, behind his back, somebody was ever-speaking speedwise, a powerful duckspeak which arrowed thru the usual oversound of the room.

Syme pushed away his bowl, uptaked his piece of bread in a careful hand and his cheese in the other. He toothed his bread hungerful and feeded a few mouthfuls.

'It's a beautyful thing, vaporizing...' Syme speaked, with teacherful feelings. His thin unlightful face had become lifeful, his eyes were joyspeakful and nearwise dreamful. 'Don't you understand the beauty of that, Smith? It was BB's think,' he plussed as a post-think.

A vaporful heartfulness moved over Smith's face at the word *BB*, but Syme speedwise finded that Smith was unoverjoyful.

'By year50—ante-year50, maybe,' Syme speaked. 'The oldspeak books will exist only as newspeak books, not only changed into something unsame, but changed into something opposite.'

'Changed into something opposite?' Smith questioned.

'Changed into something opposite,' Syme answered. 'All thinking will be *un*thinking. Goodthink is not thinking—not needing to think. Goodthink is unthinkful.'

Someday, Smith thinked speedwise and feeled deepwise, Syme will be vaporized. He is overknowing. He's watchful, overclearful and overspeakful. The Party doesn't enjoy those persons. Someday he will vaporize. It's writed in his face.

Smith had feeded his bread and cheese. He turned sideways in his chair to drink his coffee. At the table on his left the loud man was ever-speaking.

A youthful girl, who was sitting with her back to Smith, was heartfulwise OKing everything he speaked. Time-to-time Smith catched some words: 'I think you're pluscorrect. I cothink you, doubleplus,' speaked the youthful and unthinkful girl. But the duckspeaker never stopped, even when the girl was speaking.

Smith knowed the man was in some important position in Ficdep. He was about age30, with a strong throat and a big moveful mouth. He was head-up, and his eyeglasses catched the light and flashed to Smith blank rounds instead of eyes. The sound that outstreamed from his mouth was words—'the final end to Goldstein'—outspeaked plusspeedwise and all in 1 piece, a solid line of words, a quack-quack-quacking duckspeak. He denounced Goldstein, crimethinkers, and workstoppers. He blasted enemy warcrimes; he upspeaked BB and war heros. Whatever it was, everyword of it was pure goodthink, pure Party. Smith watched the uneyeful face with the jaw moving speedwise up-down: it was an unthinkful sound.

Syme was unspeakful for a second. The speaker at the other table duckspeaked speedwise, hearable tho the cafe was overloud. 'Duckspeak,' speaked Syme, 'It's 1 of those blackwhite words that have opposite meanings.'

Unquestion, Syme will be vaporized, Smith rethinked. He thinked it with an unjoy, tho plusknowing that Syme doubleplusdisenjoyed him and was fullwise able to denounce him as a crimethinker, if he watched or knowed Smith's ownlifeful thinks. There was something untrue about Syme. There was something unexisting: a careful coldness, an unthinkful thinking. He was goodthinkful, he thinked about Orders of the Party, he luved BB, he extrajoyed over wins, he doubleplusunluved ungoodthinkers, with truewise extraheart and up-to-date info, which other Party member unknowed.

Yet there was something ungoodnameful about Syme. He speaked things that were gooder to unspeak, he readed overplus books, he goed to the Chestnut Tree, the drinking-place of painters and musicers. It wasn't unlawful—not even an unwrited law—to go to the Chestnut Tree, yet the place was ungoodluck. The denounced leaders of the Party goed there, ante-cleanups. Goldstein had sometimes been there, doubleplusoldtime. Syme's future was undifficult to forecast. But, if Syme knowed Smith's unwatched thinking, he would denounce him speedwise to Thinkpol. Anybody and everybody would. Extraheart was unenough. Goodthink was unthinkful.

Syme upwatched. 'Here comes Parsons.' Parsons, Smith's cohabiter at Winful House, was moving thru the cafe—a plusunthin, midsize man with a frogface. At age35 he was unthin at neck and waistline, but his moves were speedful and youthful. He was a youth growed big. Tho he was wearing Party coveralls, it was nearwise unpossible to unthink of him in the blue pants, white shirt, and red necktie of the Spys, doing a commwalk or physed.

He joyspeaked 'Hello, hello!' and sitted at the table. His face was light-red. Syme had a piece of paper with a long list of words and was reading it with an ink-pencil between his fingers.

'Working during mealtime,' speaked Parsons, pushing Smith. 'Plusworkful! What've you there? Something overbrainful for me, I think. Smith, speak to you? I'm questioning about that sub you disremembered to give me.'

'Which sub is that?' questioned Smith, auto-tracking for money.

'Unluv Week. You know—house-by-house. I'm the numberer for our building. We're going all-out—doubleplusbig! Winful House will have the biggest flags on the whole street. $2 you pledged me.'

Smith finded and handed him $2. Parsons writed in an unbig notebook, in the orderful handwriting of an unwriter.

'Otherwise, I hear that my unbig youth gunned you with his toy ante-day. I gived him an earful. I speaked to him: I'll take the gun away if he redoes it.'

'I think he was unjoyful about ungoing to the execution.'

'Shows the correct spirit, doesn't it? Playful unbig youths they are, both of them, and goodthinkers! All they think about is Spys, and the war. D'you know what my girl did ante-day06, when her troop was commwalking? She coleaved the commwalk with 2 other girls and followed an unusual man. They tracked him for 2 hours thru the woods, and then, when they returned to the city, they handed him over to Thinkpol.'

'What did they do that for?' questioned Smith, semi-shocked.

Parsons respeaked, prideful and crimestopful. 'My girl thinked he was an enemy agent—maybe dropped by airplane, for example. But here: What do you think maked her question him? She watched him, and he was wearing unusual shoes—she'd unwatched anybody wearing those shoes. So it's possible he was an outsider. Thinkful, for a youth age07!'

'What happened to the man?'

'I don't know about that. But I wouldn't be shocked if...' Parsons maked the hand-move of gunning, and clicked his tongue for the bang.

'Good,' speaked Syme, unthinking, unupwatching from his piece of paper.

'We mustn't be unsafe,' Smith OKed, dutyful.

'The war...' speaked Parsons.

As tho to verify this, a trumpet-call streamed from the telescreen overhead. But it wasn't an update about winning the war; only a newscast from Miniplenty:

'Everybody!' loudspeaked a heartful youth. 'Attention, everybody! We have plusgoodnews for you. We're winning the war for production! Production of consumer goods upped our lifestyles plus 20% over ante-year. Allover Oceania workers marched out of factorys and offices in crowded unplanned AM demos, and paraded thru the streets with flags, thanking BB for our new joyful lifestyle, which his thinkful leadership has gived us. Here are some of the numbers. Feed...'

The Miniplenty trueword 'our new joyful lifestyle' respeaked a few times. Parsons, his attention catched by the trumpet-call, heared seriouswise with an open mouth, nearsame a sleepful mid-schooler. He was unable to follow the numbers, but he knowed they were satisfying. Smith unopened his ears to the unnearer sounds and heared the news that outstreamed the telescreen. There had been unplanned demos to thank BB for upping the chocolate ration to 20g. Did he, Smith, remember that ante-day it was broadcast that the ration would be *downed* to 20g a week? Parsons disremembered it; Syme doublethinked it. Smith was single, ownlifeful.

The doubleplusgood stats outstreamed the telescreen. Compared to ante-year, there was plus feed, plus wear, plus houses, plus furniture, plus cookpots, plus gas, plus boats, plus helicopters, plus books—plus everything, except unhealth, crime, and unsane. Year-by-year and minute-by-minute, everybody and everything was zipping speedwise up.

But Smith was unjoyful about his lifestyle. Always his bellyfeel was unOK, bellyfeeling that something was unexisting. It was true: he disremembered anything unsame. So why should he overfeel it, unless he had some ante-memory that things had been unsame?

He rewatched the persons in the cafe. He thinked that everybody else was beautyful, even if they unweared the uniform blue coveralls. The goodest body-type of the Party—tall strong youths and big-breast girls, blondhair, lifeful, sunful, carefree—existed and was maybe even the majority. It was the type that growed goodest under the leadership of the Party.

The Miniplenty update ended on another trumpet-call. Parsons speaked, overjoyed by the numbers, 'Miniplenty's gooder this year,' with a knowing shake of his head. 'Otherwise, Smith, you have any razors you're able to give me?'

'None,' speaked Smith, untrue. 'I've been using the same razor for 6 weeks.'

'Only thinked I'd question you.'

The duckspeaking from the near table, stopped during the update, had restarted, ever-loud. The girl had semi-turned round and was watching him. It was the blackhair girl.

She was side-watching him, but with unusual fireful eyes. The second she catched his eye, she turned away. The sweat started on Smith's back. A terrorful sharp unjoy arrowed thru him. It goed speedwise, but it leaved an ever-worry behind. Why was she watching him? Why did she ever-follow him? He disremembered if she had been at the table when he comed there or post-comed there. But ante-day, during 2minUnluv, she had sitted behind him, maybe to watch him and know if he was underspeaking.

His ante-think returned to him: maybe she wasn't Thinkpol, maybe she was a volunteer spy, which was doubleplusbiggest unsafe. He unknowed how long she had been watching him, maybe 5 minutes, and it was possible that he facecrimed. The unbiggest facecrime would unmask him. Nerveful shaking, unthinkful worry, self-speaking—any unbig unusual thing, anything ownlife.

The girl returned to the duckspeaker. Maybe she wasn't following him, maybe it was ungoodluck that she sitted near him today and ante-day. Syme folded up his piece of paper and inpocketed it. Parsons restarted speaking:

'Did I ever speak about,' he joyspeaked, 'the time when my youths fired the freemarket-woman's wear because they watched her wrapping meat in a poster of BB? Tracked her down and fired her. Fired her doubleplus, I think. Unbig and youthful, but sharp as razors! That's the goodest prepping they give them in Spys—gooder than in my youth. What d'you think's the newest thing they've gived them? Ear trumpets for hearing thru doors! My unbig girl bringed it ante-day—used it on our door, and she was able to double-hear inside our room. It's only a toy, remember, but gives 'em the correct mindfulness.'

The telescreen blasted the trumpet-call for rework. The mans jumped to join the line to the uppers.

chapter06

Smith was writing in his daybook:

It was 3 ante-years. Post-worktime, in an unbroad sidestreet near the Tube station, she was standing in a doorway, under an unlightful streetlight. She had a youthful face, doublepluspainted. It was the paint that maked me sexcrimeful, the white of it, nearsame a mask, and the plusred lips. Party womans never paint their faces. Nobody was on the untelescreened street. She wanted $2...

It was overdifficult to write. He unopened his eyes and pressed his fingers to them, attempting to blank the memory that reshowed. He wanted to doubleplusloudspeak a line of plusunclean-words. Or to bang his head on the wall, to kickover the table, and throw the inkpot thru the window—to do any powerful or loud or unjoyful thing that would blackout the memory.

His ungoodest enemy, he thinked, was his nerve system. At any second the overtight worry inside him maybecome facecrime. He thinked of a man in the street a few ante-weeks; a plususual man, a Party member, age35 to age40, tall and thin, carrying a workcase. The man's face was speedwise misshaped by a bodyful microshake: speedful but malhabitful. He remembered thinking: that facecrimer will be vaporized, but his facecrime was maybe unthinkful, nearsame sleepspeaking. There was noway of crimestopping that, he thinked.

He inbreathed and writed:

I goed with her thru the doorway and thru a backyard and into a sublevel kitchen. There was a bed and a light on the table, plusunlightful. She...

He was worryful. He wanted to belch. Sametimewise with the woman in the sublevel kitchen he thinked of Katharine, his ex-spouse. He remembered and rebreathed the uncold malairful smell of the sublevel kitchen, a smell of bugs and unclean wear and doubleplussexcrimeful scent—sexthinkful, because Party womans were unscented. Only the proles used scent. In his mind the smell of it was tied to extramarryful sexcrime.

It was his sexcrime01 in about 2 ante-years. Sexcrime dealing was outlawed, but it was a law that he sometimes breaked. It was unsafe, but it was undifficult. The unmoneyed districts were crowded with sexcrime dealers, prepped to freemarket themselfs. Some would deal for a bottle of harddrink. Sexcrime dealing was unimportant, if it was underhanded and unjoyful and only with prole womans. The true crime was sexcrime with Party members. All intermarrying of Party members must be OKed by committee, and the only reason to marry was to produce Party youths. Goodsex was teached to every Party member, starting in youth. Youth Antisex League pushed for 100% antisex and youths born from Artsem and teached in Reclaimcens. It was goodthink for Party womans.

He rethinked of Katharine. It was unusual how he thinked of her only sometimes. For somedays he disremembered that he had been marryed. They had been together only 15 months. Katharine was a tall woman, plusstraight, with doubleplusgood body-moves. She had a birdface, a face maybe true or prideful, and he finded there was only goodthink in her mind. She was able to indrink all Party truewords and Orders. *The Soundtrack* he othernamed her, in his mind. He would have stayed with her except for 1 thing—sexcrime.

If Smith wanted sexcrime, she would pullback and harden. When he touched her, she was nearsame a wood doll, pulling him to her and sametimewise pushing him away. It was doubleplusshameful and ungood, so he stopped. He was OK with antisex. But Katharine wanted goodsex. She had 2 names for it: 'making a baby' and 'our duty to the Party'. They must, she thinked, produce a youth if they were able to. But no youth was born, and they parted.

Smith outbreathed, nonspeakful. He reupped his pen and writed:

She throwed herself on the bed, and speedwise, unprepping, in the straightest, ungoodest way I'm able to think of, offed her wear. I...

He rewatched standing in the unlight, the smell of bugs and sexcrimeful scent in his nose, and a dissatisfyed feeling in his heart, which was mixed with the memory of Katharine's goodsexful white body. Why was it always this way? Why was he unable to have a spouse instead of unclean sexcrime dealers? But it was nearwise unthinkable. Party womans were ever-same. Goodsex was as deep in them as Party trueheart. By careful teaching as youths, by games and cold water, by the Orders loudspeaked at school, Spys, and Youth League, by speaks, parades, songs, truewords, and military music, sexcrimethinkful feeling was blanked from them. Party womans were unbreakable, but he wanted to breakdown that wall of goodsex with sexcrime. Sexcrime was antiParty crimethink.

But he must write the whole story:

I upped the light. When I watched her in the light...

Post-unlight, the unstrong light of the light had been pluslightful. It was time01 to overwatch the woman. He had stepped to her and then stopped, sexcrimeful and terrorful. He was unjoyful of exposing himself as a sexcrimer by coming here. It was possible Thinkpol would stop him: they maybe waiting outside the door. If he leaved ante-sexcriming...!

He had speedwise watched the woman: *oldwoman*. The paint was deep on her face, nearsame a mask. There was some white in her hair; but the truewise terror was her open mouth, showing only a holeful black. She had no tooths.

He speedwrited, in scratchful handwriting:

She was an oldwoman, plus age50. But I sexcrimed with her.

He repressed his fingers to his eyelids. He had writed it, but he was unchanged. The mind-game had been unuseful. The wanting to doubleplusloudspeak unclean-words was ever-strong.

chapter07

Smith writed:

The proles are 85% of the Oceania population.

He remembered walking down a crowded street, and a plusbig loudspeak of womans had bursted from a sidestreet. It was doubleplusbig, terrorful, and unjoyful. A deep loud 'O-o-o-o-o!' His heart jumped. He goed there and watched a crowd of 200 or 300 womans crowding round freemarketeers, with faces as unjoyful as persons on an underwatering boat. A freemarketeer had been dealing metal cookpots. They were ungood, malproduced things, but the supply had speedwise stopped. The winful womans with their cookpots, banged and pushed by the others, were attempting to leave. An outburst of loudspeaks when 2 unthin womans holded the same cookpot and attempted to outpull it from each other's hands. They were both pulling, and then the handle breaked off. Smith watched them, disgusted. Why were they unable to loudspeak about something important?

He writed:

Proles and animals are nearsame.

That, he thinked, maybe Party trueword. The Party had stopped ever-work and undermoney for the proles. Ante-Revolution they had been doubleplusunder the freemarketeers, overhungered and hammered. Womans had been overpowered to work in coal mines, youths dealed to factorys at age06. But, doublethink, the proles were underpersons who must stay down. It was unneeded to know about the proles. If they ever-worked, their other acts were unimportant.

By themselfs, nearsame cows in the field, the proles had returned to a self-true lifestyle. They were born, they growed up in the streets, they started work at age12, they had an unlong flowertime of beauty and sexcrimes, they marryed at age20, they were mid-age at age30, they unlifed about age60.

Overwork, the care of houses and youths, unbig wars with cohabiters, movies, sports, harddrink, and the Lottery fulled their world. To ever-control them was undifficult. Thinkpol agents ever-watched them, spreading untrue news storys and stopping unsafe persons; but the Party unattempted to teach them Orders or goodthink. The Party unwanted them as members, only as unthinkful Party persons, who would be OK with longer workhours or unbigger rations. The doubleplusbig majority of proles had telescreens in their houses. Goodsex was unpushed on them. Sexcrime was unstopped, unmarry was OK. They were sub-questioning.

Smith downed his hand and carefulwise scratched his dishealthful leg. He always returned to the unpossible: truewise knowing about ante-Revolution lifestyles. He outdrawered a schoolbook copy he had getted from Parsons, and started recopying words into his daybook:

Ante-Revolution, the city wasn't as beautyful as today. It was an unlight, unclean, unjoyful place where nearwise nobody had enough feed and 100,000 unmoneyed persons without boots on their foots or roofs over their heads. Youths must work 12 hours a day for coldhearted overpowers, who hammered them if they worked overunspeedwise and feeded them only bread and water. But the moneyed persons had doubleplusbig beautyful houses with 30 servers. These moneyed persons were called freemarketeers. They were unthin, unbeautyful persons with stonefaces, nearsame the picture on the opposite page, wearing a long blackcoat and an unusual tube-shape hat, which was called a tophat. This was the uniform of the freemarketeers, and nobody else was OKed to wear it. The freemarketeers dealed everything in the world, and everybody was their workers. They dealed all the land, all the houses, all the factorys, and all the money. If anybody unfollowed the freemarketeers, they stopped them and disworked them, overhungered them. When any person speaked to a freemarketeer, they must downwatch and unwear their hat...

How did he know if it was true? It *maybe* true Oceania persons were gooder now than ante-Revolution. The only counter-evidence was unspeaked, in his bones, an animalthink overfeeling about his lifestyle: sometime things had been unsame. He thinked about his coldhearted, unsafe lifestyle now; he feeled unfull, unclean, and halfhearted. Life was unsame the telecasts outstreaming the telescreens. For Smith, hours and days and months were unlifeful and over-usual: working overtime, pushing into the Tube, repairing an outweared sock, underhanding sugar. The Party wanted everything doubleplusbig and doubleplusnew—a world of metal and concrete, overbig machines and terrorful bombs—warrers and single-minders, comarching, same-thinking and loudspeaking truewords, ever-working, -warring, -winning—300,000,000 persons all sameface.

Smith was dissatisfyed. He downed his hand and rescratched his leg. The telescreens fulled his eyes and ears, AM-PM, with stats evidencing that persons now had plus feed, plus wear, gooder houses, gooder rec—longer lifes, unlonger workhours; were bigger, healthfuller, stronger, joyfuller, knowfuller than persons 50 ante-years. It was unable to be evidenced or disevidenced, and so, on-and-on, doublethinkful. Everything outwhited, nearsame vapor.

The past ever-changed for Smith. The biggest feeling—an ungooddream— was never clearwise understanding why the plan was undertaked. The good of rectifying the past was clear, but the final reason was unknowed. He reupped his pen and writed:

I understand HOW: I disunderstand WHY.

Smith thinked, as he had manytimes ante-thinked, that he was unsane, a minority of 1. Was it an unsane sign to think the past was unrectifyable? He maybe single in thinking that, and if single, then he was unsane. But being unsane unworryed him doubleplus: the terror was that it maybe untrue.

He upped the schoolbook and watched the BB picture on the front. The deep eyes watched his own. A plusbig power downpressed him—something goed inside his skull, terrorful, hammering his brain, reasoning with him, to disthink the evidence of his eyes. Blackwhite, the Party would speak: $2 + 2 = 5$. And he would cothink it. It was unavoidable. Goodthink was blackwhite. And maybe correct. How did he know $2 + 2 = 4$? or the law of gravity? or the past was unchangeable? If the past and the world existed only in his mind, and if his mind was controllable—what then?

But no! His heart speedwise changed. O'Brien's face, not remembered for any clear reason, had streamed into his mind. He knowed that O'Brien was on his side. He was writing the daybook for O'Brien—*to* O'Brien: it was nearsame a long message which nobody would read, but it was writed to 1 person.

The Party speaked blackwhite: disthink the evidence of your eyes and ears. It was their final importantest order. He was downhearted as he thinked of the oversize power of the Party; any goodthinker would overthrow him in conversation, with sharp arguments he was unable to understand, unable to answer. But he was correct! They were untrue and he was true. The unthinkful must be safeguarded, hold onto that! Stones are hard, water is wet, unupholded things drop to the ground. He feeled that he was speaking to O'Brien and writing something important:

$2 + 2 = 4$. If that's true, everything else follows.

chapter08

From somewhere coffee smell outstreamed to the street. Smith auto-stopped. For maybe 2 seconds he was returned to the half-remembered world of his youth. Then a door banged, knifing the smell speedwise, as tho it was a sound.

He had walked a few km thru the prole-district streets, and his dishealthful leg was ungood. This was time02 in 3 weeks he had ungoed CommcenPM: an uncareful act, because the number was carefulwise watched. By Orders, a Party member had no extratime, and was never single, except in bed. When he was offwork, he should be in some commrec: self-walking was ownlife. But when he outed Minitrue post-work, the summerful month04 sky was an uncold blue and speedwise he overfeeled ownlifeful.

Unthinking, he turned away from the Tube station and walked into the maze of the city, south, then east, then renorth, unwatched in unknowed streets and unworryed which way he was going.

The proles are 85% of the Oceania population, he had writed in the daybook. The words returned to him, speaking true of an otherworld he wanted to touch. The prole district was a world-within-a-world: robbers, sexcrime dealers, drug-pushers, and freemarketeers. He was somewhere in the district northeast of the Tube station, walking thru a street of unbig houses with outweared doorways, nearsame holes. There was plusunclean water here-and-there on the street, and persons crowded in shocking numbers, in-and-out of unlightful doorways, up-down unbroad sidestreets—flowerful girls with red-painted mouths, and youths who tracked down the girls, and big unspeeding womans, and unshoed youths in holeful wear, who played together.

Persons unwatched Smith; but a few eyed him with a safeguarded interest. 2 overbig womans with forearms folded atop their bellys were speaking outside a doorway. Smith catched pieces of their conversation:

"'Ye',' I spe'ks t'er, "tha's'll pl'sgood," I spe'ks. "Bu'f y'd a be'n m' place y'd a done th' same's wha' I done. 's 'ndiff'ult to'cize," I spe'ks, "bu' y' ain' go' a same prob'ems wha' I go'.'"

'A',' speaked the other woman, 'tha's j'st it. Tha's j'st where it's.'

The loudspeakers stopped speaking and watched him. But it wasn't unluvful, only careful, a speedful hardening, nearsame facing some unknowed animal. The Party blue coveralls was unusual on this street, and it was enough to get the attention of Thinkpol. Thinkpol would stop him if they watched him. 'Show us your ID. What are you doing here? What time were you offwork? Is this your usual route?'

Speedwise, the whole crowd was comoving. There were loudspeaks from allsides. Persons runned into doorways. A woman outed a doorway ahead of Smith, uptaked a doubleplusunbig youth playing in the street, and reinned the doorway: all in 1 move. Sametime, a man in black wear outed a sidestreet and runned to Smith, arrowing excited at the sky.

'Steam'!' he loudspeaked. 'Watchout! Bang over'ead! Down speedfu'!'

Steamer was prolespeak for rocket bomb. Smith speedwise self-throwed to the ground. The proles were nearwise always correct when they speaked about rocket bombs. They had some animalthink which ante-speaked to them, tho the rockets travelled speedfuller than sound. Smith holded his forearms overhead. A blast moved the street up-down; unheavy things hitted his back. When he standed, he was covered with glass from the nearest window.

The bomb had blanked a house-group 200m up the street. Black dust in the sky, white dust in the air, a crowd round the houses. There was an unbig pile in the street ahead of him, and something plusred mid-pile. He walked to it: a person's hand, knifed at the wrist, bloodful. He kicked the thing into the street.

To avoid the crowd, Smith turned at a sidestreet. Within a few minutes, he outed the block where the bomb had dropped, and the sexcrimeful crowds on the streets were ongoing, as tho nothing had happened. It was nearwise 20:00, and the prole drinking-places were crowded with harddrinkers. Out the doors, ever-opening and -unopening, comed the smell of toilets, wooddust, and unsweet harddrink. At a housefront, 3 mans were standing together, 1 was holding a folded newspaper; the others reading over his shoulder, deep attention in every line of their bodies. It was clear they were reading a serious news story. Speedwise, the group breaked up and 2 of the mans were in a powerful argument, near warful.

'C'n' y' f'ck'n' 'ear wha' I spe'k? N' num'er end' 'n se'en ain' win' fo' 'ver fou'een mon's!'

'Ye' i' 'as 'en!'

'N', i' 'as n't! A' 'ome I go' th' 'ole lo' o' 'em fo' 'ver t'o ye' wri' d'n 'n a pi' a pap'. I ta' 'em dow' reg'la' a the clo'. An' n' num'er end' in se'en...'

'Ye', a se'en 'as win'! I near' know t' f'ck'n' num'er. Fo'-oh-se'en, it end' 'n. 't were 'n mon'oh-t'o—sec'n'wee' 'n mon'oh-t'o.'

'Mon'oh-t'o?! I go' 't a' do'n 'n bla' 'n' whi' 'n' th're's n' num'er...'

'O, pa' 't 'n!'

They were arguing, redface, about the Lottery. The proles gived serious attention to the Lottery, with its everyweek dealout of money. For 1,000,000s of proles the Lottery was their biggest unthinkful joy, their drug, their mind-upper. For Lottery stats, persons who only under-readed and -writed were able to do complex numbering and shocking acts of memory. There was a subgroup who dealed systems, forecasts, and goodluck signs. Everybody in the Party knowed the winners of big money were unpersons. Only unbig money was winned by the proles.

The sidestreet downhilled. He feeled that he had ante-walked in this houseblock and a bigger street was near. From somewhere ahead there comed loudspeaking. The street turned sharpwise and ended in stairs to a substreet, where a few freemarketeers were dealing feed. Smith remembered where he was. This sidestreet leaded to another street and, 5 post-minutes, the freemarket where he had dealed the blank-book, now his daybook. And in another near unbig freemarket he had dealed the penholder and ink bottle.

He stopped at the stairs. On the opposite side of the street there was an unclean unbig drinking-place, windows coated with dust. An oldman, unstraight but healthful, with a white mustache, opened the door and inned. Smith watched him and thinked that the oldman, maybe age80, had been mid-age during the Revolution. He was a connection to the ante-Party end-world of over-freemarkets. The words from the schoolbook he had copied into his daybook returned to Smith's mind, and unsane-thinking overtaked his mind: Go into that drinking-place, meet that oldman, and question him. 'Speak to me about your youthful life. How was it in those days? Were things gooder than now? Or were they ungooder?'

Speedwise, so he unbecomed terrorful, he downstaired and crossed the unbroad street. It was unsane. It was a plusoverunusual act. If Thinkpol questioned him, he would speak untrue about his unhealth, but they would maybe stop him.

He opened the door, and the cheeseful smell of unsweet harddrink hitted him in the face. The loudspeaking dropped to about half-sound. He feeled everybody eyeing his blue coveralls. A game at the otherside of the room stopped for about 30 post-seconds. The oldman was arguing with the server: a big strong youthful man with oversize forearms. A group, standing round with glasses in their hands, was watching.

'I a'st y'u cor'ct en'ugh, di'n't I?' speaked the oldman, straightening his shoulders, warful. 'Y' ain' g't a pin' glas' 'n t' 'ole f'ck'n' b'oze'?'

'N' wha' 'n 'ell's n'me 's a pin'?' speaked the server, leaning on the table with his fingerends.

'Ark a' 'im! Cal's 'issel' a s'rve' 'n' don' kno' wha' a pin' 's! Y, a pin' 's t' 'alf 'f a quar', 'n' th're 's fo' quar's t' t' g'llon. 'Ave t' te'ch y' t' A, B, C nex'!'

'Neve' 'ear'd 'f 'em,' speaked the server. 'Lit' 'n' 'a'f-lit'—tha's 's all we s'rve. Th're 's t' glass' 'n t' shel' 'n fron' y'.'

'I l'vs a pin',' respeaked the oldman. 'Y' cou'd 'a pul'd m' a pin' 'ndif 'icul' 'n'ugh. We di'n' 'ave thes' f'ck'n' lite's w'en I's a 'uthfu' man.'

'W'en y' wer' a 'outhfu' man we w're 'll livin' 'n t' tre'tops,' speaked the server, watching the other harddrinkers. There was loud joyspeaking, and the worry caused by Smith's inning unexisted. The oldman's whiteface reddened. He turned away, self-speaking, and banged into Smith. Smith catched his arm, gentlewise.

'May I get you a drink?' he questioned.

'Y' 're a gen',' speaked the other, restraightening his shoulders. He had unwatched Smith's blue coveralls. 'Pin'!' he plussed overstrong to the server. 'Pin' 'f wal'op.'

The game was in full replay, and the group of mans started speaking about the Lottery. Smith was disremembered for a second. There was a table underwindow, where he and the oldman were able to speak, unterrorful of being overheared. It was unsafe, but the drinking-place was untelescreened.

'You've watched doubleplusbig changes from when you were a youthful man,' speaked Smith, questioning.

The oldman's uncolorful blue eyes moved to the gameboard, round the room, and to the toilet, as tho thinking the drinking-place showed the changes.

'T'har'dr'nk w's good'r. And big'r! When I's a 'uthfu' man, 'nstr'ng har'dr'nk w' 4p a pin'. Tha's 'nte-wa'.'

'Which war was that?' questioned Smith.

'I's 'll wa's,' speaked the oldman, unclearwise. He upped his glass, and his shoulders restraightened. 'Ere's y' t' pl's good's' of 'ea'th!'

'You are doubleplusolder than I am. You are able to remember ante-Revolution. Persons of my age don't truewise know anything about those times. We're able to only read about them in books, and the books maybe untrue. I want to hear your thinking on that. The history books speak about ante-Revolution lifestyles: doubleplusunsame from now. Doubleplusungoodest, persons underfoot, unlaw, unmoney. Ungooder than anything we're able to think of. Here in the city, persons never had enough feed, whole-life. Half of them were unshoed. They overworked 12 hours, outed school age09, slept 10 in a room. And sametime a few persons, only

1,000—the freemarketeers—were moneyful and powerful. They ownlifed everything that there was to deal: doubleplusbig beautyful houses with 30 servers, airplanes, and goodest harddrink, they weared tophats…'

The oldman joyed speedwise.

'T'p 'ats! 'nus'al y' sh'u'd spe'k o' 'em. T' sam't'ing come int' m' 'ead on'y ant'day, I dono 'y. I w's jest th'nkin', I ain' watched t'p 'ats in 'ears. Gorn ou', t'y 'ave. T' final time I w'ar'd 'ne w's a' m' sis'-'n-law's. An' tha' w's…I'm 'nab'e t' gi'e y' t' d'te, bu' 't must'a b'en 50 'nte-'ears.'

'The tophats are unimportant,' speaked Smith, patienceful. 'But these freemarketeers—they and a few lawers who helped them—were the leaders of the world. Everything existed for them. You were their workers. They were able to do whatever they wanted with you. They sended you anywhere, nearsame cows. They were able to sexcrime any girls they wanted. You must off your hat. Every freemarketeer goed about with a server group who…'

The oldman rejoyed.

'Bugs! I s'met'mes go t' t' par' t' 'ear t' mans spe'kin'—'ll t'pes t're w's. And t're w's 'ne man—I'm 'nab'e t' gi'e y' 'is n'me, bu' a pow'rfu' spe'k'r 'e w's. E 'alf giv' 't 'em! "F'ck'n' t' le'd'rs!"—tha' w's anot'r of t'm. An' 'y'n's—'e c'll'd 'em 'y'n's.'

Smith feeled they were speaking crosswise.

'What I truewise wanted to know was: Do you feel you have gooder lifestyle now than you had in those days? The moneyed persons, the persons at the top… My question is: Were these persons able to down you underfoot, because they were moneyed and you were unmoneyed? Is it true, for example—I'm only quoting what I've readed in history books—that you must unwear your hat for them?'

The oldman thinked deep. He drinked his harddrink ante-answer.

'Ye' t'y w'nt'd y' t' t'uch y'r 'at t' 'em. I's c'rr'ct. I 'nthink' 't, bu' I d'ne 't m'nyt'me', m'sta'.'

A dispowerful feeling taked hold of Smith. The oldman's memory was only a waste-pile of unbig things. All-day questions would unget any true info. The Party history maybe true: maybe even doubleplustrue. He maked a final attempt.

'Maybe I haven't been clear. What I'm attempting to speak about is this: You've been lifeful pluslongtime; your half-life was ante-Revolution. In year25, for example, you were growed up. From what you're able to remember, was life in year25 gooder than now, or ungooder?'

The oldman watched thinkfulwise the gameboard. He drinked his harddrink, plusunspeedwise. He speaked open-mindful and thinkful, as tho the harddrink had gentled him.

'I kno' wha' y' 'nte-t'nk m' t' spe'k. Y' 'nte-t'nk m' t' spe'k 's I'd be rey'thful. P'rsons 'd spe'k t'y'd be y'thful, if y' arst 'em. Y'g't y'r 'ea'th an' stron' wh'n y're y'thful. Wh'n y' g't t' m' t'me o' l'fe y' ain' n'ver go'd.'

The oldman speedwise unsitted and speedwalked to the unscentful toilet on the otherside of the room. Smith sitted for a minute at the window, watching his unfull glass. It was unuseful to stay cospeaking. The man remembered 1,000,000 unuseful things, but important things were outside his memory. Proles were nearsame bugs, which are able to watch unbig things but not big things. His foots recarryed him to the street. He thinked, the doubleplusbig and undifficult question, 'Was life gooder ante-Revolution or now?' was answerable even now, because the records were rectifyed—the speak of the Party goodering lifestyles was true.

His thinking stopped speedwise. He stopped and upwatched. He was on an unbroad street, with a few unlightful unbig freemarkets and houses. Overhead, 3 uncolorful metal balls which had been gold. He knowed this place! He was standing outside the freemarket where he had dealed the daybook.

A feeling of terror goed thru him. It had been a crimeful act to deal the book, and he had pledged never to recome near the place. But the millisecond that he unthinked, his foots had auto-returned him here. He had hoped to crimestop, but he was unable to self-safeguard.

It was nearwise 21:00, but the freemarket was open. He feeled that he was watched outside on the street, but unwatched inside, so he stepped thru the doorway. If Thinkpol questioned him, it was possible to speak about an attempt to deal razors.

The dealer had turned on an overhead light. He was maybe age60, unstrong and unstraight, with a long nose and gentle eyes, misshaped by eyeglasses. His hair was nearwise white, but his eyebrows were bushful and black. His eyeglasses, his over-careful moves, and his old blackcoat: he was nearsame a bookwriter or a musicer. He was unloud, as tho outwhited, and his prolespeak was upper than the majority of proles.

'I recognized you on the street,' he speaked speedwise. 'You're the gentleman that dealed the woman's memory-book. That was a beautyful piece of paper, that was. There hasn't been paper nearsame that for—50 ante-years.' He watched Smith over the top of his eyeglasses. 'Is there anything I'm able to do for you? Or did you only want to...?'

'I was walking,' speaked Smith, unclearful. 'I only inwatched. I don't want anything...'

'I don't think I'm able to satisfy you.' He maked a hand-move, sheepful. 'This is how it is: an unfull market. Between you and me, dealing in old stuff is nearwise ended. Nobody wants it, and no supply. Furniture, glass bowls, metal cookpots: it's all been breaked and fired.'

The doubleplusunbig inside of the market was overfull, but everything was nearwise unimportant: round the walls were unnumbered dustful pictureframes; in the window, trays of metal pieces, outweared hammers, breaked penknifes, unworking clocks, and otherwise mixed-waste; on an unbig corner table a pile of interesting stuff. As Smith walked to the table his eye was catched by a round, smooth thing that flashed gentle in the light, and he upped it.

It was a heavy glass piece, unstraight on 1 side, flat on the other, nearwise a half-ball. The color and the feel of the glass was soft, unusual, rainwaterful. At the heart of it, bigger under the unstraight glass, a light-red, complex-spiral, nearsame a flower.

'What is it?' questioned Smith, plusinterested.

'That's an *ocean flower* that is. From the ocean…they inbedded them in glass. That's age100…or plusage100.'

'It's a beautyful thing,' speaked Smith.

'It's a beautyful thing,' respeaked the other, thankful and joyful. 'But there's not many that'd know it.' He coughed. 'Now, if it happened that you wanted to deal it, that'd be $4. I'm able to remember when that thing would have dealed for $8, and $8 was…I'm unable to renumber it, but it was big money. But who cares about old things now?'

Smith speedwise dealed and inpocketed the thing. He overwanted it; it speaked to him with beauty and feelings of a time plusunsame from now. The soft rainwater glass wasn't glass that he had ante-watched. The thing was doublebeautyful because it was unuseful, tho he thinked it had been used as a paperweigher. It was plusheavy inpocket, but goodluckful it unoutshaped his pocket. It was an unusual thing, a crimeful thing, for a Party member to have. Anything oldthink, anything beautyful, was always questionable.

The oldman was plusjoyful post-dealing $4. 'There's another room upstairs...There's furniture in it...only a few pieces. I'll get a light, if we're going upstairs.'

He getted the light, and, with unstraight back, leaded Smith, unspeedwise, up the angled and outweared stairs, along a doubleplusunbroad hallway, and into a room, which unfaced the street and faced the backyard and roofs. The furniture was floorplanned for the room to be inhabited: a carpet piece on the floor, a few pictures on the walls, and a deep disorderful armchair near the fireplace. An oldtime clock with a 12-hour face was clicking away on the overshelf. Underwindow, and fulling nearwise quarter-room, was an oversize bed and mattress.

'We inhabited here until my spouse unlifed. I'm dealing the furniture. Now, that's a beautyful wood bed, or it would be, if you're able to out the bugs. But maybe you'd find it overbig, overheavy.'

He was highlighting the whole room, and in the uncold unlightful light the place had an unusual ante-joyful feel. The think speedwise moved thru Smith's mind: it would be plusundifficult to deal the room, if he was strongheartful. It was animalful, unpossible. He attempted to crimestop when he thinked it; but the room had unsleeped in him an ante-memory. He knowed the feel of sitting in this room, in an armchair beside a fireplace, with his foots up and a coffeepot on the stove; 100% ownlife, nobody watching him, no loudspeaker tracking him. Unsoundful, except the coffeepot song and the clock clicking.

'No telescreen!' he was unable to crimestop lowspeaking.

'A, I never had those things, and I never feeled the need of it. Now, that's a nice table in the corner there. Tho you'd need to repair it, if you wanted to use it.'

There was an unbig bookshelf in the other corner, and Smith gravityed to it, but finded no crimethinkful books. Tracking-down and rectifying books was 100% in the prole districts. There unexisted anywhere in Oceania a book printed ante-year60. The oldman, carrying the light, was standing in front of a picture in a wood frame, on the otherside of the fireplace, opposite the bed.

'Now, if you happen to be interested in old prints...' he speaked carefulwise.

Smith goed to the metal picture of an oval building with square windows, an unbig tower in front, and a statue behind. Smith watched it for a few seconds. He maybe knowed it, but he disremembered the statue.

'The frame's connected to the wall,' speaked the oldman, 'but I'll disconnect it for you, maybe.'

'I know that building,' speaked Smith, post-thinking. 'It's in plusdisrepair now. It's mid-street, outside the Law Courts.'

'That's correct. Outside the Law Courts. It was bombed in...O, many ante-years.' He joyfaced, sheepful and knowing that he speaked something unthinkful, and plussed: 'Oranges and lemons!'

'What's that?'

'O...*Oranges and Lemons* was a song we had when I was a youth. How it goes, I disremember, but I do know it ended, "Here comes a candle to light you to bed, Here comes a knifer to knife off your head." It was a game. We outed our arms for you to go under, and when we ended "Here comes a knifer to knife off your head" we downed our arms and catched you.'

Smith thinked unclearwise about the age of the Law Courts. It was ever-difficult to number the age of a city building. Anything big and important, if it was near-new, was post-Revolution, and anything clearwise older was from the unlightful Mid-Ages. The time of the freemarkets produced nothing important. He was unable to learn history from buildings, samewise he was unable to learn it from books. Statues, in-writed words, memoryful stones, street names—anything that maybe throwed light on the past had been system-rectifyed.

Smith undealed the picture. It was unusualler and crimethinkfuller than the glass paperweigher, and unpossible to carry, unless it was unframed. But he stayed for a few minutes, speaking to the oldman, whose name wasn't Weeks—as he had thinked from the name overwindow of the market—but Charrington. Charrington, maybe, was age63 and had inhabited this market for 30 years. He had planned to rectify the name overwindow, but had never done it.

While they were speaking, the half-remembered song was running thru Smith's head. He thinked that post-month, he would recome to the market and reavoid CommcenPM. The serious uncrimestop had been returning, post-dealing the daybook, and unknowing if the freemarketeer was cocrimeful. But...! Yes, he rethinked, he would return. He would deal pieces of beautyful waste. He would deal the metal picture of the oval building, unframe it, and bring it back, unwatched, under his coveralls. He would pull the whole song from Charrington's memory. The unsane think of dealing the upstairs room reflashed speedwise thru his mind.

He leaved Charrington upstairs and downstaired single, so the oldman was unable to watch him counterspying the street, ante-outing the door, but for maybe 5 seconds, overjoy maked him uncareful, and he outstepped, speedwise, unante-watching thru the window. He had started the song: 'Oranges and lemons…'

Speedwise his heart turned to ice and his belly to water. A person in blue coveralls was coming down the street, 10m away. The girl from Ficdep, the blackhair girl. The light was downing, but it was undifficult to recognize her. She watched his face, straightwise, then walked on speedwise, as tho she had unwatched him.

For a few milliseconds Smith was unable to move. Then he turned right and walked away, unspeedful, unwatching. He was going the uncorrect way. The question was now answered: the girl was spying on him. She had followed him here, because it wasn't by luck that she was walking sametime on the same backstreet, a few km from any district where Party members inhabited. It was doubleplusungoodluck. If she was a Thinkpol agent, or a volunteer spy acting self-important, it was the same: she was watching him now and had watched him go into the drinking-place also.

It was difficult to walk. The glass piece inpocket banged his thigh at each step, and he was half-minded to outpocket it and throw it away. The ungoodest thing was his belly unjoy. For a few minutes he feeled that he would unlife, if he unfinded a toilet. But there weren't public toilets in this prole district. Then the bodyful micro-shakes stopped, leaving an unsharp unjoy.

The street ended. Smith stopped, standed for a few seconds thinking unclearwise what to do, then turned round and started to rewalk. He thinked that by running he would catch the girl. He would track her, until they were in some uncrowded place, and then hammer her skull with a stone. The glass piece inpocket was heavy enough. But he crimestopped speedwise, because he was unstrong. He was unable to run, he was unable to hit her. She was youthful and sportful and would safeguard herself. He thought also of speeding to Commcen and staying there until the place unopened, to have some semi-counterevidence. But that was unpossible. He was unenergized. He wanted to return to Winful House speedwise, sit down, and be unloud.

It was post-22:00 when he returned to his room. The lights would be off at 23:30. He goed into the kitchen and drinked a cupful of harddrink. Then he goed to the table, sitted, and outdrawered the daybook. But he unopened it. From the telescreen a woman blasted out a Party song. He sitted watching the daybook cover, attempting to stop the words in his mind.

He was shocked by his unuseful body: terrorful and unmoving, iced solid when he needed to act. He would have stopped the blackhair girl, if he had acted speedwise, but he was dispowered. Crimethinking, he self-warred with his own body. Even now, tho harddrinking, the unsharp unjoy in his belly disordered his thinking. Life was self-war, second-to-second: hungerful, cold, unsleepful, unsweet bellyfeel.

He opened the daybook. It was important to write something. The telescreen woman started a new song that flashed into his brain nearsame arrows of breaked glass. He attempted to think of O'Brien, for/to who Smith was writing the daybook, but he started thinking about Thinkpol. Thinkpol would stop him, with the usual questions. He would answer: loudspeaking. The end was always the same. Nobody was unwatched, and nobody unanswered the questions. Post-crimethink, he must be crimestopped and vaporized.

He reattempted to picture O'Brien's face. 'We'll meet in the place where there's no unlight,' O'Brien had speaked to him. He knowed what it meaned, or thinked he knowed. The place where there's no unlight was a possible future, which he would never watch, but he was able to forecast it, and cohabit that otherworld.

With the telescreen ever-speaking, he was unable to follow his series of thinks. The face of BB comed into his mind, displacing O'Brien. Same as he had done a few ante-days, he outpocketed a coin. BB's face upwatched him, heavy, unexciteful, safeguarding: but what joyface was under the black mustache? Nearsame a gray-sound, the truewords recomed at him:

FOREVER AT WAR
JOYFUL IN WORK
STRONG IN PARTY

part02

chapter01

It was mid-AM, and Smith outed his cubicle to go to the toilet.

A single person was coming from the otherside of the long, lightful hallway. It was the blackhair girl. 4 ante-days, she had been outside the freemarket. Now she comed nearer, her right arm dishealthful, supported and strapped to her coveralls. Maybe she had breaked her hand while turning the big kaleidoscopes where Ficdep books were writed.

The girl was about 4m away, when she misstepped and dropped flat on the floor. A sharp loudspeak of unjoy comed out of her. She had downed on the dishealthful arm. Smith stopped. The girl had upped to her knees. Her face had changed to white-yellow color. Her mouth outstanded redder. Her terrorful eyes were watching his.

An unusual feeling moved in Smith's heart. In front of him was an enemy who was attempting to kill him; in front of him, also, was a person, unjoyful and maybe with a breaked bone. Animalthinkful, he had moved to help her. When he had watched her hit the dishealthful arm, he feeled the unjoy in his own body.

'You're dishealthful?' he questioned.

'It's nothing. My arm. It'll be OK in a second.'

She speaked as tho her heart were shaking. Her face had uncolored.

'You haven't breaked anything?'

'No, I'm OK. It dishealthed me for a second, that's all.'

She upped her other hand to him, and he helped her up. She had recolored and was healthfuller.

'It's nothing,' she respeaked. 'I only gived my wrist a bang. Thanks!'

And she walked away, speedful, as tho it had truewise been nothing.

The whole event taked a half-minute. Avoiding facecrime was a learned habit, nearsame animalthink, and they had been standing in front of a telescreen when the thing happened. But it had been difficult to unbetray a speedful shock, for while he was helping her up, the girl placed something, unwatched, into his hand. It was something unbig and flat. As he walked into the toilet, he inpocketed it and feeled it with his fingerends. It was a piece of paper folded into a square: a message. He wanted to read it speedwise, but the telescreens ever-watched.

He returned to his cubicle. Unserious, he throwed the piece of paper on the desk with other papers, reweared his eyeglasses and pulled the speakwrite to him. '5 minutes,' he self-speaked, '5 minutes!' His heart banged in his breast, terrorful loud, but the workpiece he was doing was usual, rectifying a long list of numbers, unneeding 100% attention. What was writed on the paper? He thinked there were 2 possibles:

01. The girl was a Thinkpol agent. He unknowed why Thinkpol would message him that way, but maybe they had their reasons. It maybe a threat, a callup, a self-kill order, a trick.

02. The message uncomed from Thinkpol, but from some underground organization. Maybe the Brotherhood existed! Maybe the girl was part of it!

His heart banged, and it was difficult to speakwrite his numbers. He rolled up the workpieces and inned them newtube. 8 post-minutes. He reweared his eyeglasses, outbreathed, and pulled in a pack of workpieces, with the piece of paper on it. He flattened it. In big unshaped handwriting:

I UNLUV BB I LUV U

For a few seconds he was overshocked, unmoving, unable to memory-hole the crimethinkful thing. He plusknowed it was sexcrimeful, but he was unable to crimestop. He rereaded it.

It was difficult to work. He was unable to think, but he unfacecrimed in front of the telescreen. He bellyfeeled fire. Mealtime in the uncold, crowded, loud cafe was unjoyful. He had hoped to be single during mealtime, but Parsons sitted beside him, overpowerful, and speaked streamwise about prepping for Unluv Week. He was overjoyed by a cardboard statue of BB, 2m broad, which his girl's Spy troop was making for Unluv Week. In the loud cafe, Smith was unable to hear Parsons and ever-speaked for his unthinkful words to be respeaked. He onetime watched the blackhair girl, at a table with 2 other girls. She unwatched him, and he unrewatched her.

Post-mealtime was OK. A careful, difficult workpiece—rectifying a series of production reports from 2 ante-years, to unname an important Inner Party member—taked a few hours and sidelined everything else. This was the work that Smith was good at, and for 2 hours the blackhair girl was out of his mind. Then the memory of her face returned, and an uncontrolled overfeeling to be ownlife. Single in his room, ownlife, it maybe possible to full think about the message.

Ante-CommcenPM, he speed-feeded a healthful meal in the cafe, speeded to Commcen, speaked with a conversation group, played games, drinked a few glasses of harddrink, and heared a half-hour speak: *The Party and Boardgames.* His mind spiraled, but it wasn't until 23:00, when he was in bed—in the unlight, where he was unwatched by the telescreen, if he stayed unspeakful—that he was able to rethink about the words *i luv u.*

A question that must be answered: how to contact the girl and plan to meet? He thought it was unpossible she was tracking him. He knowed it was untrue, because of her clear terror when she handed him the message. Her eyes had been terrorful. Sexcrimestopping never crossed his mind. Only 5 ante-days, he had dreamed about hammering her skull with a stone. He thought of her naked, youthful body, as he had dreamed about it. He had thinked she was a goodthinker, nearsame all Party members, headful of unluv for crimethinkers, bellyfeel for BB, but truewise she was a sexcrimer.

Dishealthful terror taked him as he thinked the white youthful body maybe speed away from him, she maybe change her mind if he uncontacted her speedwise! But meeting was overdifficult. It was nearsame attempting to win a game when he had ante-unwinned. Whichever way he turned, the telescreen faced him. He had thinked of all possible ways to contact her, 5 post-minutes the message; but now, with ownlifetime, he rethinked them 1-by-1, as tho placing knifes in a row on a table.

They were unable to remeet in Recdep, and he unknowed where Ficdep was in the Minitrue building, and unreason for going there. If he knowed her housenumber, and the time she offworked, he would plan to meet her somewhere; but waiting outside Minitrue and following her was unsafe, because it was ever-watched. Sending a message was out of the question: he unknowed the girl's name. Final, he thinked the safest place was Recdep cafe. If he was able to meet her single, at a table somewhere mid-room, not overnear the telescreens, and with loud conversation everywhere—it maybe possible to exchange a few words.

For the post-week, life was nearsame an unsleepful dream. Post-day, she inned the cafe as the end-trumpet sounded and he was leaving. Maybe she had been changed to a later worktime. They uncowatched. On the doublepost-day, she inned the cafe at the usual time, but sitted with 3 other girls under a telescreen. Then, for 3 terrorful days, she was unthere. His whole mind and body was overfeeling, gelful. Every move, every sound, every contact, every word that he must speak or hear, was doubleplusunjoyful. He dreamed about her. He untouched the daybook during those days. His work was unexciteful, and he was able to sometimes disremember her for 10 minutes. What had happened to her? He was unable to question that. She maybe vaporized, she maybe self-killed, she maybe replaced to otherside of Oceania: doubleplusungoodest, she maybe changed her mind and was avoiding him.

Post-day, she recomed to the cafe. Her arm was rehealthful. Smith was over-excited and unable to crimestop watching her for a few seconds. Doublepost-day, he nearwise speaked to her. When he inned the cafe she was sitting at a table, single. It was unlate, and the place unfull. The line moved, then stopped, because somebody in front was getting sugar tablets. But the girl was ever-single, when Smith taked his tray and started walking to her table, unserious, his eyes watching a place at the table behind her. He was maybe 3m from her, 2 post-seconds, then someone speaked behind him: 'Smith!' He acted as tho unhearing. 'Smith!' the man respeaked, louder. It was unpossible. He turned round.

A youthful man named Wilsher, an underknowed coworker, was arrowing, with joyface, to an unfull place at his table. It was unsafe to ungo. Post-recognized, he was unable to go and sit with a single girl. It was overwatchable. He sitted with an unenemyful joyface. Wilsher's unthinkful face joyed into his. Smith daydreamed of hammering that face with a sharp hammer.

The girl's table fulled a few post-minutes, but she had watched him coming to her, and maybe she understanded his plan. Post-day, he was careful to go to the cafe unlate. She was single, at a table in the same place. The person ahead of him in the line was an unbig, speedwise-moving, bugful man with a flatface and doubleplusunbig, questionful eyes. As Smith turned with his tray, he watched the unbig man walking straight to the girl's table. His hopes redowned. There was an unfull place at a table unnearer, but Smith thinked the unbig man was self-attentionful and would sit at the unfullest table. With ice in his heart Smith followed. A doubleplusbig crash: the unbig man was outspread on the floor, his tray had dropped, stew and coffee overstreaming the floor. He upstanded and malwatched Smith, who he clearwise thinked had tricked him. But it was OK. 5 post-seconds, with a bursting heart, Smith was sitting at the girl's table.

He unwatched her. He unpacked his tray and speedwise started feeding. It was all-important to speak speedwise, but terror holded him. She had speaked to him post-week. Now, she maybe changed her mind, she *had* changed her mind! It was unpossible to sexcrime; those things unhappened. He maybe would have crimestopped, but he watched Ampleforth, the poemer, walking round the room with a tray, tracking down a place to sit. Ampleforth would sit at Smith's table, if he watched him here. There was maybe a minute to act. Smith and the girl were feeding, unchangeful. The stuff they were feeding was a stew of white beans. Smith started lowspeaking. They unupwatched; unchangeful, they spooned the waterful stuff into their mouths, and between spoonfuls exchanged a few words in unfeelful lowspeaks.

'What time do you offwork?'

'18:30'

'Where're we able to meet?'

'The Square, near the statue.'

'It's plustelescreenful.'

'That's OK, if there's a crowd.'

'Any sign?'

'No. Come to me only when I'm with other persons. And unwatch me, stay somewhere near me.'

'What time?'

'19:00'

'OK'

Ampleforth unwatched Smith and sitted at another table. The girl and he unrespeaked. They were sitting on opposite sides of the same table, but they uncowatched. The girl speed-feeded and leaved; Smith stayed.

Smith was in the Square ante-19:00. He walked round the base of the oversize BB statue, which watched the south skys where he had overpowered enemy airplanes in the War of Airfield01. At 19:05 the girl was unthere. The terror retaked Smith. She was uncoming, she had changed her mind! He walked unspeedwise to northside Square. The girl was standing at the statue base, reading, or unreading, a poster. It was unsafe to go near her. Telescreens were all-round the base. Loudspeaking and heavy trucks were coming from somewhere to the left. Speedwise everybody was running thru the Square. The girl speeded round the statue base and joined the crowd. Smith followed. As he runned, he heared some loudspeaking about truckfuls of POWs.

Persons were crowding southside Square. Smith—who usualwise gravityed to the outer edge of overcrowds—pushed, hitted, spiraled into mid-crowd. He was nearing the girl but was stopped by an oversize prole man and an oversize prole woman, a bodyful wall. Smith moved sideways and, with a powerful jump, shouldered between them. It feeled as tho strong hips were grinding him to dust, but then he had breaked thru, sweating. He was plusnear the girl. They were shoulder to shoulder, both straight-watching to the front.

A long line of trucks, with flatface safeguards armed with machineguns standing in every corner, was going unspeedwise along the street. Unbig mans in outweared green uniforms were sitting, overcrowded, in the trucks. Truckfuls-and-truckfuls of the unjoyful faces outwatched over the trucksides. Smith knowed the POWs existed, but he watched them only on-and-off. The girl's shoulder and arm were pressed to his. Her cheek was near his; it was uncold. She speedwise taked the lead, as she did in Recdep cafe. Unshowful, she started lowspeaking, with lips undermoving, sometimes overpowered by loudspeakers and the deepsound of trucks.

'Are you able to hear me?'

'Yes'

'Are you able to offwork day07?'

'Yes'

'Then hear this carefulwise. You must remember this. Go to the Tube station…'

In militaryspeak that shocked him, she outlined the route that he should follow. Half-hour Tube travel; turn left outside the station; 2km along the street; a gate with top board unexisting; a foot-track thru a field; an overgrowed street; a foot-track between bushs; an unlifeful tree. It was as tho she had a map in her head.

'Are you able to remember all that?' she lowspeaked, final.

'Yes'

'You turn left, then right, then releft. And the gate has no top board.'

'Yes. What time?'

'About 15:00. Wait there. I'll go there another way. You remember everything?'

'Yes'

'Then leave now, as speedful as you're able.'

But he was unable to out speedwise from the crowd, which was unsatisfyable and open-mouth, watching the line of trucks. Party members in the crowd loudspeaked, disjoyful, but the proles were interested: outsiders were unusual animals, watched only sometimes and speedwise as POWs, warcrimers, going to execution or joycamps. The round faces were uncleaned, unrazored, and over-unfulled. Their eyes watched Smith's, sometimes with unusual fire, and then flashed away. The line of trucks was near the end. In the final truck he watched an oldman, his head and face covered with grayhair, standing with wrists crossed in front of him, as tho they were strapped. It was nearwise time for Smith and the girl to part. But at the final second, overcrowded together, her hand feeled for his and gived it a speedful touch.

It was only 10 seconds, but it feeled a longtime that they holded hands. He thinked that he unknowed the girl's eye color. They were maybe brown, but persons with blackhair sometimes had blue eyes. Turning his head and watching her was unsafe. With hands together, unwatched by the crowd of bodys, they straight-watched, frontwise and unchangeful, and instead of the girl's eyes, the unjoyful eyes of the old prisoner watched Smith.

chapter02

Smith walked unspeedwise up the street, thru light and shadow, outstepping into gold places, wherever the trees opened. Under the trees to the left, the ground was covered, vaporful, with flowers. The air kissed his skin. He was sexcrimethinkful. It was day02 month05. From somewhere deeper in the heart of the woods comed birdsongs.

He was unlate. Travel had been undifficult, and the girl was clearwise knowledgeful, so he was unterrorful. Maybe she was able to find an unwatched-place. He unfeeled safer in the country. No telescreens, but always watchful mics to hear and recognize him; it was difficult to travel single and avoid attention. Thinkpol at Tube stations watched Party members, with difficult questions. But no Thinkpol stopped him, and walking from the station he was 100% careful, backwatching that he was unfollowed. The Tube was overstreaming with an oversize crowd of proles, from an untoothful doubleante-parent to a baby, everybody joyful because of the summerful weather, out to the country to deal freemarket feed.

The street broadened, and he comed to the foot-track the girl had speaked of, which dropped between bushs. He had no clock, but it was ante-15:00. The blue flowers were so plentyful underfoot that it was unpossible to unwalk on them. He downed and started taking them, thinking he would give flowers to the girl when they meeted. He had collected some and was smelling their scent when a sound at his back iced him: a foot breaking unbig branchs. He retaked other blue flowers. It was the goodest thing to do. It maybe the girl, or maybe he was followed. To stop was to show shame. He taked another-and-another. A hand gentle-touched his shoulder.

He upwatched. It was the girl. She shaked her head, a sign that he must be unspeakful, then opened the bushs and speedwise leaded the way along the unbroad foot-track into the woods. Clearwise she had ante-walked this way, for she sidestepped the wet places by habit. Smith followed, holding his flowers. He was excited, but as he watched her strong thin body, moving in front of him, with the red waist-tie tight round her waist, her round hips, he feeled low and heavy. He thinked that when she turned round and watched him she would pull away. The sweet air and the green leafs disheartened him.

On the walk from the station, the month05 sun maked him feel unclean and over-white, an inside animal, with the black dust of the city in his skin. He thinked that she had unwatched him in the sunlight, in the open. They comed to the downed tree that she had speaked of. The girl jumped over it and parted the bushs, making an opening. Smith followed her to an open space in the woods, a doubleplusunbig grass hill rounded by tall youthful trees. The girl stopped and turned, 'Here we are.'

He was facing her, yet he was underhearted to move nearer to her.

'I unwanted to speak in the street,' she speaked. 'There's maybe a mic there. I unthink there is, but maybe. Always possible those pigs recognize us. We're OK here.'

He was underhearted to touch her. 'We're OK here?' he respeaked, unthinkful.

'Yes...all these trees!' They were unbig trees, which at sometime had been knifed down and regrowed into youthful trees. 'There's nothing big enough for a mic. And I've ante-sexcrimed here.'

They were only making conversation. He had moved nearer to her. She standed in front of him plusstraight, with a big joyface, thinking about why he was speaking but unacting. The flowers had self-dropped to the ground. He holded her hand.

'Until this second, I unknowed your eye color.' Smith watched her eyes. They were brown, light-brown. 'Now that you've watched *me*, outside and truewise, are you able to ever-watch me?'

'Yes'

'I'm age39. I've a spouse that I'm unable to leave. I've a dishealthful leg and ungood tooths.'

'I'm uncareful and sexcrimeful,' speaked the girl.

The post-second, she was in his arms. He feeled 100% distrue, dreamful. Her youthful body was pressing to his own, her blackhair was in his face, and yes! she had upturned her face and he was kissing the broad red mouth. Her arms were round his neck, she was calling him 'luv.' He pulled her to the ground, she was unsexcrimestopping, but he was unable to do what he wanted with her. He touched her body, but he was unsexcrimeful. He stayed joyful that it was happening, but he unsexcrimed. It was overspeedful, her youth and beauty were terrorful, he was overhabitful of life without womans—he unknowed the reason. The girl upped herself and pulled a flower from her hair. She sitted with him, placing her arm round his waist.

'Never mind, luv. We have the whole day. Isn't this a doubleplusgood unwatched-place? I finded it when I was offtrack on a commwalk. If anybody comes we'll hear them 100m away.'

'What's your name?'

'Julia. I know yours. It's Smith, 6079 Smith.'

'How did you find that?'

'I think I'm gooder at finding things than you are, luv. What did you think of me, that day I gived you the message?'

He unwanted to speak untrue to her. It was luv-giving to start with the ungoodest.

'I disluved you. I wanted to rape you and then kill you. 2 ante-weeks, I thinked seriouswise of hammering your head with a stone. If you want to know, I thinked that you were with Thinkpol.'

The girl joyspeaked, joyful, clearwise hearing it as evidence that her mask was doubleplusgood.

'Thinkpol! You thinked that, true?'

'Maybe not. But you're youthful and sportful and healthful—I thinked that maybe...'

'You thinked I was a good Party member. Goodthinkful in word and act. Flags, parades, truewords, games, commwalks—all that stuff. And you thinked that I'd inform on you as a crimethinker and get you killed?'

'Yes, something of that type. Doubleplusmany youthful girls are nearsame that, you know.'

'It's this f'ckin' thing that does it,' she untied the red Youth Antisex League waist-tie and throwed it into a tree. Then, as tho touching her waist had reminded her of something, from her coveralls she outpocketed an unbig chocolate pack. She halfed it and gived a piece to Smith. He knowed by the smell that it was plusunusual chocolate. It was in paper. Sometime, he had chocolate nearsame this piece. The scent had upped some memory, which he was unable to remember, but it was powerful and worrying.

'Where did you get this stuff?'

'Freemarket,' she answered, ungoodthinkful. 'Speaking true, I'm that type of girl. I'm good at games. I was troop-leader in Spys. I do volunteer work for Youth Antisex League. Hours-and-hours I've handed out their f'ckin' waste allover the city. I ever-carry the flag in parades. I'm ever-joyful and I never avoid anything. Always loudspeak with the crowd, that's what I learned. It's the goodest mask for crimethink.'

The chocolate uniced on Smith's tongue. It was joyful. But there was that memory moving round the edges of his mind, something strong-feeled but unshaped, nearsame something watched from the corner of his eye. He pushed it away from him, knowing only that it was the memory of some act which he wanted to undo, but was unable to undo.

'You're doubleplusyouthful. Why were you watching me?'

'It was something in your face. I thinked it was possible. I'm good at finding persons who are outsiders. When I watched you I knowed you were anti*them*.'

Them meaned the Party, the Inner Party, who she downmouthed with a disluv that worryed Smith, tho he knowed they were unwatched. Her speak was shockful. Julia was unable to speak of the Party without using low, unclean-words. He enjoyed it. It was another sign that she was counterRevolution.

They had leaved the open space in the woods and were rewalking thru the on-and-off shadows, with their arms round each other whenever the foot-track was broad enough to walk side-by-side. He touched her waist and feeled it was soft, untied by the red waist-tie. They only lowspeaked. At the woods-edge she stopped him.

'Don't out to the field. There maybe somebody watching. We're OK if we stay behind the trees.'

They were standing in the shadows of the bushs. The sunlight, coming thru unnumbered leafs, was plusuncold on their faces. Smith outwatched the field, and undergoed an unusual, unspeedful shock, recognizing it from his dreams: the field with a foot-track going thru it, here-and-there. In the bushs on the opposite side, the trees moved in the wind, their leafs nearsame woman hair. Smith thinked there was an unwatched stream near here, with fish swimming in greenwater.

'Isn't there a stream somewhere near here?'

'That's correct, there's a stream. It's at the field-edge. There're fish in it, doubleplusbig. You're able to watch them in the water under the trees, moving their tails.'

'It's Gold Country—nearwise,' he lowspeaked.

'Gold Country?'

'It's nothing true. A landscape I've watched sometimes in a dream.'

'There...!' lowspeaked Julia.

A bird landed on a branch 5m away, nearwise at the level of their faces. Maybe it had unwatched them. It was in the sunlight, they in the shadows. It outspread its wings, refolded them carefulwise, downed its head for a second, as tho worshipping the sun, and then started outstreaming song. In the unsoundful woods, the sound of the song was shocking. Smith and Julia coholded, plusinterested. The music goed on-and-on, minute-by-minute, with doubleplusbig changes, unsameful resonging, as tho the bird were showing off. Sometimes it stopped for a few seconds, outspread and inspread its wings, then bigged its colorful breast and resonged. Smith watched, with an unclear semi-worship. For who, for what, was the bird songing? Nothing was watching it. Why sit at the woods-edge and song its music to nothing?

He thought, is there a mic somewhere near? He and Julia had only lowspeaked, and it would unhear them, but it would hear the birdsong. Maybe at the otherside of the mic, some unbig, bugful man was watching, serious—hearing *that*. But unspeedful the music outed everything from his mind, a liquid stuff that streamed allover him and mixed with the sunlight coming thru the leafs. He stopped thinking and only feeled. The girl's waist in his arms was soft and uncold. He pulled her to him; her body was uniceful. Wherever his hands moved, she was all as smooth as water. Their mouths togethered; it was plusunsame the hard kisses they had ante-exchanged. When they moved their faces away, both of them outbreathed deep. The bird heared them and flyed away with a loud sound of wings.

Smith placed his lips to Julia's ear. '*Sexcrime.*'

'Not here. The unwatched-place. It's safer.'

Speedwise, sometimes breaking unbig branchs underfoot, they returned to the open space in the woods. When they were inside the round of trees, she turned and faced him. They were cobreathing speedful, but rejoyfaceful. She standed watching him for a millisecond, then pulled the zipper of her coveralls. And, yes! nearwise his sexcrimeful dream. Speedwise, she unweared her coveralls and side-throwed them, with a move which was able to undermine a whole civilization. Her body flashed white in the sun. But he unwatched her body;

his eyes were pulled to her light-brown face: strong, heartful, spirited, joyful. He downed in front of her and taked her hands in his.

'How many times have you sexcrimed?'

'100 times, or plus.'

'With Inner Party members?'

'Not with those pigs, no. There's plenty that *want* to, but they're goodsexful.'

His heart jumped. She had sexcrimed 100 times; he wanted it to be 1,000 times. Anything unlawful ever-fulled him with an animal hope. If he was able to blast the whole Party with sexcrimeful dishealth, he was joyful to do it! Anything to waste away, to dispower, to undermine the Party! He pulled her down so they were face-to-face.

'Hear this: I luv you, I luv sexcrimes, I luv your sexcrimes. Do you understand that?'

'Yes, 100%.'

'I unluv the pure, I unluv the good! I unwant any goodthink to exist anywhere. I want everybody to be unlawful in the heart.'

'Then you'll luv me, luv. I'm unlawful in the heart.'

'You luv doing this? I don't mean me; I mean sexcrime itself?'

'I luv it.'

That was what he wanted to hear. He pressed her down in the grass, in the flowers. The sexcrime was undifficult. Later, the up-down of her breasts returned to usual speed, and they untogethered, joyful. The sun was plusuncolder. They were both sleepful. He getted her coveralls and semi-covered her. Speedwise they slept, and slept for about a half-hour.

Smith unsleeped. He upsitted and watched her light-brown face, sleeping, pillowed in her hand. Except for her mouth, she was unbeautyful, with lines round her eyes, unlong blackhair, plussoft. He unknowed her true name or where she inhabited.

The doubleplusyouthful strong body, now unpowerful in sleep, unsleeped in him a shameful, safeguarding feeling. But the unmindful gentle that he had feeled under the tree, while the bird was songing, unreturned. He opened her coveralls and watched her smooth white body. A man watched a girl's body, and it was sexcrimeful, and that was the story-end. It was antiParty sexcrime. It was politcrime.

chapter03

'We're able to recome here another time,' speaked Julia. 'It's safe to use any unwatched-place 2 times. But not for a few post-months.'

When she unsleeped, she had becomed watchful and workful, reweared her coveralls, retied the waist-tie, and started planning for their return travel. She was sharp-mindful and hands-on, which Smith wasn't, and she had militaryful knowledge of the country round the city, remembered from unnumbered commwalks. The route she gived him was unsame his outful route, and bringed him to an unsame Tube station. 'Never return the sameway you leaved,' she speaked, an important Order from Spys. She would leave, and Smith should leave post-half-hour.

She named a place where they were able to remeet 4 post-days, post-work: a street in an unmoneyed district with a freemarket which was crowded and loud. She would be dealing, tracking down new boots or something. If she thinked they were unwatched, she would touch her nose when he was near her; otherwise he should walk by, unrecognizing. But with goodluck, mid-crowd, it was safe to speak for a quarter-hour and plan another meet.

'And now I must go,' she speaked when he had understanded it. 'It's my duty to return at 19:30 for 2 hours at Youth Antisex League, handing out booklets, or some f'ckin' thing. Give me a cleanup, would you? Do I have any flowers in my hair? Everything's OK? Then goodbye, my luv, goodbye!'

She throwed herself into his arms, kissed him, powerful, and post-second pushed thru the trees and into the woods, shadowful and unsoundful. Even now he unknowed her name or housenumber. But it was unimportant. They never returned to that unwatched-place in the woods.

During month05, they resexcrimed in another unwatched-place knowed to Julia, a tower in near-unfull country, where a newtype bomb had dropped 30 ante-years. It was a good unwatched-place, but going there was plusunsafe.

Otherwise, they meeted only in the streets, in an unsame place every PM and always unlongtime. In the street it was usualwise possible to speak, unfacecrimeful. As they streamed thru the crowded streets, not side-by-side and uncowatching, they had an unusual on-and-off conversation, which clicked on-and-off nearsame the light of a lighthouse, speedwise knifed into unspeak by a Party uniform or a telescreen, then restarted post-minutes mid-sentence, then speedwise knifed as they disconnected, then restarted post-day. Julia was plushabitful with this conversation type, which she othernamed 'speaking in pieces.' She was also shockful good at speaking with lips unmoving.

During a PM meet, they were walking unspeakful down a sidestreet when the world jumped, an overloud blast, and the air blacked. Smith was laying on his side, terrorful. A rocket bomb had dropped plusnear. Speedwise, he watched Julia's face a few cm from his, doublepluswhite, as white as paper. Even her lips were white. She was unlifeful! Her face was deep-coated with stuff, and dust on her his lips. He pulled her to him and kissed her uncold face: lifeful.

Other PM meets, they walked by each other, unsignful, because Thinkpol comed round the corner or a helicopter flyed overhead. Even if it was safe, it was difficult to find time to meet. Smith's workweek was 60 hours, Julia's overtime was longer, the press of overwork changed, and manytimes their offworkdays were unsame. Julia goed to speaks and demos, handed out booklets for Youth Antisex League, prepped flags for Unluv Week, collected for the savings plan. It was her mask. If she followed the unbig laws, she was able to break the big laws. She speaked to Smith about volunteering for the overtime work done by extraheartful Party members. So, everyweek, Smith overworked 4 hours hammering together unbig metal pieces, maybe rocket-bomb parts, in a cold-air underlighted factory, where the knocking of hammers mixed, unlifeful, with the music of the telescreens.

When they meeted in the unwatched tower, the blanks in their conversation were fulled up. It was a doubleplusuncold day. The air in the unbig square room was plusuncold, unmoving, and smelled overpowerful of bird waste. They sitted speaking for hours on the dustful pile of branchs on the floor, upping time-to-time to outwatch the windows and know that nobody was coming.

Julia inhabited a dorm with 30 other girls. 'Always the smell of womans! How I unluv womans!' She enjoyed working on Ficdep book-writing machines, running and repairing a powerful and over-complex electric motor. She was 'unthinkful,' but enjoyed using her hands and was good with machines. She speaked about the whole process of writing a book: from Plancom order to final touchup by Rewrite Squad. But she was uninterested in the endproduct. She 'unenjoyed reading.' Books were things that must be produced, nearsame boots or cookpots.

Julia disremembered anything ante-year60s, and the only person she knowed who speaked sometimes of ante-Revolution was an ante-parent, who was vaporized when she was age08. At school, she was head of a sports team and winned physed 2 years in series. She was a troop-leader in Spys and branch-leader in Youth League ante-joining Youth Antisex League. She had always masked a doubleplusgood-name. She had even been ordered to work in Pornosec of Ficdep (a sign of good-name, but a mask for Julia), producing sexcrimeful porn for the proles. She had stayed there for a year, helping to produce booklets—*Flashing Storys, Girls Dorm*—in packs to be dealed underhanded by prole youths, who thinked they were dealing something outlawed.

'What are these books?' questioned Smith, interested.

'O, wasteful. They're uninteresting, only 6 storys, but they change them round. I was only on the kaleidoscopes, never on the Rewrite Squad. I'm not bookful, luv—not even enough for that.' All Pornosec workers were girls. Girls were controllable, goodsexful and lawful about the waste they handled.

'The Party thinks girls should always be pure. Here's a girl who isn't, anyway.'

Her sexcrime01 was when she was age16, with a man age60, who self-killed to avoid being stopped. 'And that was good,' speaked Julia, 'otherwise they'd have learned my name from him, when he answered their questions.' There had been many other sexcrimes. Her lifestyle was plusundifficult. She wanted a goodtime; 'they'—the Party—wanted to stop her; she was unlawful as manytimes as she was able to. She thinked 'they' wanted to rob her joys and she want to avoid being stopped. She plusunluved the Party and speaked about it with the uncleanest words, but she unthinked about the Party. Except where it touched her ownlife, she was uninterested in Orders of the Party. She had unheared of the Brotherhood, and thinked it was untrue news. Any antiParty organization would be overpowered, so it was unthinkable.

They unspeaked about possible marry. The committee wouldn't OK them to marry, even if Smith was able to leave Katharine, his spouse. It was unhopeful, a daydream.

'How was she, your spouse?' questioned Julia.

'She was goodthinkful.'

'Yes, I know that type of person...'

He started speaking about his marryful lifestyle, but she ante-knowed the important parts. She speaked to him, nearwise she had watched or feeled it: the hardening of Katharine's body when he touched her, the way she pushed him away, ever-strong, even when her arms holded him tight. With Julia, it was undifficult to speak about those things.

'I would have stayed marryed, except for sexcrime.' He speaked about the ice-cold goodsex that Katharine had planned, sameday everyweek. 'She unenjoyed it, but nothing would stop her from doing it. She called it...'

'Our duty to the Party,' speaked Julia, speedwise.

'How did you know that?'

'I've been to school also, luv. Sex-speaks everymonth. And in Youth League. They hammer it into you for years. It works. But you never know; persons are blackwhite.'

With Julia, everything returned to her own sexcrimes. The way she speaked about it: 'When you sexcrime you're using up energy; and post-sexcrime you're uncareful about everything. You're unenergyful, unable to get excited about BB and 3YPs and 2minUnluv and Orders of the Party.' That was plustrue, he thinked. There was a straight connection between goodsex and goodthink.

Speedwise, his mind returned to Katharine. She would, unquestioning, have informed on him to Thinkpol, but she was overunthinkful to find his ungoodthink. The over-uncold of the day maked him remember Katharine, and he started speaking to Julia about something that happened, or unhappened, on another over-uncold summer day, 11 ante-years.

It was 3 or 4 months post-marry. They were offtrack on a commwalk somewhere. They were unspeedful, behind the others, but they turned uncorrectwise, and comed to the edge of a coal mine. It was a down-drop of 10m or 20m, with big stones at the bottom. Nobody else was there. When she knowed they were offtrack, Katharine becomed plusworryful. To be away from the loud crowd of walkers gived her an ungood feeling. She wanted to backtrack speedwise. But Smith watched some red flowers in the hole under them, and he speaked to Katharine:

'Katharine! Those flowers...down near the bottom. They're unsame colors.'

She turned to go, but she returned for a second, worryful. She even leaned over the hole to watch where he was arrowing. He was standing behind her, and he placed his hand on her waist. He thought how single they were. Nobody anywhere, nothing moving, not even a bird. Maybe there wasn't a mic, and even if there was a mic, it would only hear sounds. It was the over-uncoldest sleepfullest daylight hour. The sun fired down on them. And the think hitted him...

'Why you ungived her a good push?' questioned Julia. 'I would've.'

'Yes, you would've. I would have, if I was the same person then as I am now.'

'Are you disjoyful you unpushed her?'

'Yes. I'm disjoyful I unpushed her.'

They were sitting side-by-side on the dustful floor. He pulled her nearer to him. Her head on his shoulder, the joyful smell of her hair. She was doubleplusyouthful, he thought, she wanted something from life, she disunderstanded that killing a person wasn't the answer.

'It would unchange nothing.'

'Then why're you disjoyful?'

'Only because I want good, not ungood. In this game that we're playing, we're unable to win. Some types of unwin are gooder than other types, that's all.'

He feeled her shoulders shake with dis-cothink. She ever-opposited him when he speaked anything of this type. She unthinked persons were always overpowered. She knowed that unlater-or-later Thinkpol would stop her, but—otherwise—she thought it was possible to build an unwatched world where she was able to ownlife. All she needed was goodluck, a sharp mind, and a strong heartful spirit. It was maldoublethink. She disunderstanded there wasn't any joy. From their sexcrime01, starting a war antiParty, it was gooder to think of herself as unlifeful.

'We're unlifeful.'

'We're not unlifeful yet,' Julia speaked, clear and true.

'Not yet. 6 post-months, 1 post-year, 5 post-years...maybe. I'm terrorful of unlife. You're doubleplusyouthful, so maybe you're terrorfuller of it. Clearwise, we'll unspeed it, if we're able to. But it's unchanged. If humans stay human, unlife and life are same.'

'Untrue! Which do you want for sexcrime, me or a skeleton? Don't you enjoy life? Don't you luv feeling: This is me, this is my hand, this is my leg, I'm true, I'm solid, I'm life! Don't you luv *this*?'

She spiraled round and pressed her breasts on him. He feeled her breasts, plussexcrimeful, thru her coveralls. Her body streamed some of its youth and energy into his.

'Yes, I luv that.'

'Then stop speaking about unlife. And now, luv, we must plan our remeeting. We're able to return to that place in the woods. We've waited a longtime. But you must go there by an unsame route. I've planned it all. You take the Tube...but...I'll write it out for you.'

And in her militaryful way she pulled together a square of dust and, with a branch, started mapping it on the floor.

chapter04

Smith walked round the outweared unbig room over Charrington's market. Underwindow, the overbig bed with outweared bedcover. The oldtime clock with a 12-hour face was clicking on the overshelf. On the corner table, the glass paperweigher that he'd ante-dealed flashed low in the half-light.

In the fireplace, a hammered metal oilstove, a cookpot, and 2 cups, gived by Charrington. Smith fired the stove and onned the coffeepot. He'd bringed a pack of Winful Coffee and some sugar tablets. The clock hands showed 7:20, but it was 19:20 truewise. Julia was coming at 19:30.

'Unthinking, unthinking,' his heart ever-speaked. Knowful, unneeded, self-killful unthinking—sexcrime by a Party member was undifficult to trackdown and watch. As he had forecasted, Charrington maked dealing the room undifficult. He was clearwise joyful about the money it would bring him and unshocked that Smith wanted the room for sexcrime. Instead he side-watched and downspeaked, becoming semi-shadowful. Ownlife, he speaked, was a plusimportant thing. Everyone wanted an unwatched-place. And when they had a place, it was only correct that anyone who knowed of it should hold that knowledge. Outwhiting and unexistful, he speaked about the 2 housedoors, 1 of them at the backyard, which goed to a backstreet.

In the backyard, somebody was songing. Smith outwatched, safeguarded by his place in the room. The month06 sun was high in the sky, and in the sunful backyard, an overbig woman, solid as stone, with muscleful red forearms, was marching here-and-there between a cleaning-sink and a line, clipping a series of square white things which Smith recognized as babywear. Whenever her mouth was unfull of clips she was songing powerful:

'It was only an 'nopeful dream on a m'nth'4 dye
But a lo'k an' a word an' the dreams they moved
They 'ave tak'd my 'eart awye!'

The song had been allover the city for ante-weeks. It was 1 of unnumbered nearsame songs from Musicdep Prolefeed. The songwords were unhumanwise writed on the versifyer machine. But the woman songed songfulwise, making a joyful sound. He heared the woman songing and the sound of her shoes on the stones, and youths in the street, and unnear unloud streetsounds, and yet the room was unusualwise unsoundful, because it was untelescreened.

'Unthinking, unthinking, unthinking!' he rethinked. It was unthinkable they would be able to come here longtime unstopped. But they uncrimestopped wanting an unwatched-place that was ownlife, inside and near. For sometime post-sexcrime in the tower, it had been unpossible to plan meets. Worktime had been upped ante-Unluv Week. The overbig, complex preps were extrawork for everybody. Final, both of them had an offwork PM sameday. They planned to return to that unwatched-place in the woods.

On the ante-day, they meeted unlongtime in the street. As usual, Smith unwatched Julia as they streamed thru the crowd, but he speedwise watched her face and she was uncolorfuller than usual.

'It's off,' she unloudspeaked, when she thinked it OK to speak. 'Post-day, I mean.'

'What?'

'Post-day PM. I'm unable to come.'

'Why not?'

'The usual reason. It's started unlate this time.'

For a millisecond he was powerfulwise unjoyful. During the ante-month that he'd knowed her, the sexcrime had changed. She'd become a bodyful need, somebody that he wanted and feeled was his own. When she speaked that she was unable to come, he feeled that she was untrue to him. But now the crowd pressed them together, they misstepped, and their hands touched. Her fingers pledged sexcrime. He wanted to marry. He wanted to walk thru the streets with her, as they were doing now, but openwise and unterrorful, speaking of this-and-that and dealing stuff for their house. Overall he wanted somewhere they were able to be ownlife together, and sexcrime everytime they meeted.

Sometime post-day, he thinked of dealing Charrington's room. When he questioned Julia, she speedwise OKed it. They both knowed it was unsane, as tho they were planning to step nearer to unlife. As he sitted waiting on the bed-edge he thinked again of the Miniluv sublevels. That terror moved in-and-out of his mind. There it layed, fixed in the future, as true as 100 follows 99. He was unable to avoid it, but maybe able to move it unnearer; instead, everytime, by knowful and unneeded acts, he minused the time ante-Miniluv.

Now, speedful steps on the stairs, Julia bursted into the room. She was carrying a brown toolbox, as he'd sometimes watched her carrying here-and-there at Minitrue. He started to take her in his arms, but she distogethered herself speedwise, because she was holding the toolbox.

'Half-second, I'll show you what I bringed. Watch this!'

She dropped to her knees, opened the toolbox, and outed some wrenchs and hammers that fulled the top of it; under, a number of orderful paper packs. The pack she gived to Smith had an unusual and yet unclearwise ante-knowed feeling, fulled with some type of heavy, sandful stuff which moved wherever he touched it.

'Sugar?'

'Sugar. And here's bread—white bread, not that other f'ckin' stuff—and an unbig pot of fruit-spread. And here's milk—but watch this! This I'm truewise prideful of. I had to wrap it, because...'

But she unneeded to speak about why she wrapped it. The smell was fulling the room, a complex uncold smell nearsame a product from his youth, which he sometimes smelled even now, streaming down a hallway or outspreading itself shadowful in a crowded street, smelled for a second and then unsmelled again.

'It's coffee,' he unloudspeaked, 'coffee.'

'It's coffee. There's 1kg here.'

'How did you get these things?'

'It's all freemarket stuff. There's nothing those pigs don't have, nothing.'

Smith downed beside her. He ripped open a corner of the pack.

'Luv,' Julia speaked to him 'I want you to turn your back for 3 minutes. Go and sit on the otherside of the bed. Ungo over-near the window. And unturn round until I speak to you.'

Smith watched thru the window, careless. Down in the backyard the red-armed woman was ever-marching here-and-there between the cleaning-sink and the line. She taked clips out of her mouth and songed with deep feeling:

'They spe'k that time repai's all things,
They spe'k you're able t' always disrememb'r;

But the joys' an' the tears 'cross the years
They play with my 'eart forever!'

She knowed the whole nonthinkful song by heart. The sound upstreamed with the sweet summer air, plussongful and full of a joyful unjoy. He feeled that she would be 100% satisfyed, if the month06 PM was unending and the supply of clean wear unending, to stay there for 1,000 years. He'd unheared a Party member songing, single and unplanned. It was ungoodthinkful, unsafe, and unusual, nearsame self-speaking.

'Turn round now,' speaked Julia.

He turned round, and for a second unrecognized her. He'd truewise ante-thinked she would be naked. But she was unnaked. The change was plusshocking. She'd painted her face.

She'd freemarketed in the prole district and dealed face-paint. Her lips were deep-red, her cheeks light-red, her nose whited; even a touch of something undereye to make them lightfuller. She was doubleplusungood with face-painting, but Smith thinked it was good. He'd never ante-watched or -pictured a Party woman with face-paint. Her face was shockful gooder. With some color in the correct places she'd become beautyfuller and, overall, womanfuller. Her unlong hair and manful coveralls only plussed the change. As he taked her in his arms, the scent of flowers instreamed his nose. He remembered the half-light of that sublevel kitchen, and the woman's holeful mouth. It was the same scent that she'd used; but now it was unimportant.

'Scent!'

'Yes, luv, scent. And do you know what I'll do? I'll deal girlwear from somewhere and wear it instead of these f'ckin' coveralls. I'll wear sexcrimeful underwear and high-shoes! In this room I'll be a girl, not a Party member.'

They unweared their coveralls and jumped into the oversize bed. It was time01 to be naked with her. Ante-now, he'd been over-shameful of his thin white body, with the discolored places on his dishealthful leg. The bedcover was outweared and smooth, and the oversize of the bed shocked them. They unknowed about oversize double-beds.

Post-sexcrime, they slept. When Smith unsleeped the clock hands had moved round to near 9:00, which truewise was 21:00. He unmoved, because Julia was sleeping with her head in the angle of his arm. Her paint was on his own face and the bedcover, but a light-red highlighted the beauty of her cheekbone. Yellow sunlight from the downing sun crossed the foot of the bed and lighted the fireplace, where the water in the pot was firing speedful.

Down in the backyard the woman had stopped songing, but the unloud loudspeaks of youths instreamed from the street. He thought unclearwise if, in the blanked past, it was usual to lay in bed nearsame this, in the uncold of a summer PM, a man and a woman naked, sexcriming when they wanted, crimespeaking what they wanted, unfeeling any need to unbed, only laying there and hearing gentle sounds outside. But there was never a time when that was usual. Julia unsleeped, opened her eyes, and upped herself on her elbow to watch the oilstove.

'Half that water's vaporized,' she speaked. 'I'll up and make coffee in a second. We have an hour. What time do they knife the lights in your building?'

'23:30'

'It's 23:00 at the dorm. But I must be unlater than that...'

He unopened his eyes speedwise. She down-pressed him and spiraled her arms round him, as tho to safeguard him with her uncold body. For a few seconds he felt he was in the ungooddream which replayed from time-to-time thru his lifetime, ever-same. He was standing in front of a blackwall; on the otherside, something over-terrorful. In the dream his deepest feeling was being untrue to himself, because he truewise knowed what was behind the blackwall. Nearsame outpulling a piece of his own brain, he would be able to pull the thing into the open, but he always unsleeped, unfinding what it was; but it was connected to Julia.

The black-second of terror was half-disremembered. Feeling shameful of himself, he sitted up and leaned on the headboard. Julia outed the bed, reweared her coveralls, and maked coffee. The smell from the coffeepot was so powerful and exciteful that they unopened the window, so nobody outside smelled it and questioned them. With a hand inpocket and a piece of bread and fruit-spread in the other, Julia walked round the room, uncareful, speaking about the best way to repair the table, sitting in the outweared armchair, and watching the over-unusual 12-hour clock with a joyful open-mind. She carryed the glass paperweigher to the bed to watch it in gooder light. He taked it out of her hand, plusinterested, as always, by the soft rainwaterful glass.

'What is it, do you think?' questioned Julia.

'I think it's nothing—I mean, I think it's unuseful. That's what I enjoy about it. It's an unbig piece of history that they've disremembered to rectify. It's a message from 100 ante-years, if I knowed how to read it.'

'And that picture there,' she updowned at the opposite wall, 'is that age100?'

'Plus. I think it's age200. But it's unpossible to find the age of anything now.'

She goed to watch it. 'What's this place? I've watched it somewhere.'

'It's near the Law Courts.'

The piece of song that Charrington had teached him returned to his head, and he plussed: ' "Oranges and lemons...!" '

Shocking him, she ended the line: ' "Here comes a candle to light you to bed, here comes a knifer to knife off your head!" I disremember how it goes post-that.'

'Who teached you that?' It was the other half, a countersign.

'My ante-parent. He used to song it to me when I was an unbig girl. He was vaporized when I was age08. I think I know what a lemon was. And oranges. They're a type of round yellow fruit with an unthin skin.'

'I remember lemons,' speaked Smith. 'They existed in the year50s. They were unsweet, even to smell them.'

'I think that picture has bugs behind it,' speaked Julia. 'I'll down it and give it a cleanup someday. I think it's time to leave. I must start cleaning off this paint. F'ck! I'll also get the lip-paint off your face.'

Smith stayed bedded for a few minutes. The room was unlighting. He turned to the light and layed watching the glass paperweigher. The unending interest of the thing wasn't the ocean-flower, but the inside of the glass. It was deep but as clear as air, as tho the glass was the sky of a doubleplusunbig world with its own atmosphere. He felt he was able to go inside it and, otherwise, he *was* inside it—with the oversize bed and the wood table and the clock and the metal picture and the paperweigher itself. The paperweigher was the room he was in, and the ocean-flower was Julia's life and his ownlife, ever-stopped in the heart of this glass-world.

chapter05

Syme had vaporized. He wasn't at AM work: a few unthinking persons speaked about him. Post-day, persons unspeaked about him. Doublepost-day, Smith readed the printed list of Gamescom members on the Recdep message-board. Syme had been a member. It was nearsame—nothing had been Xed out—but it was 1 name unlonger. Syme unexisted: he had never existed.

The weather was over-uncold. In mazeful Minitrue, the unwindowful rooms stayed the same with AC, but outside the streets were fireful and the smell of the post-work Tube was doubleplusungood. Prepping for Unluv Week was full-time, and all the ministrys were working overtime. Military parades, meets, speaks, movies, telecasts: all must be organized; statues builded, truewords writed, songs versifyed, storys outspreaded, photos rectifyed. Julia's section in Ficdep was unproducing books and speeding out warcrime booklets. Smith overworked, everyday going thru *The Times* ante-records and rectifying and upwriting news storys which were to be quoted in speaks. Late PM, when crowds of uncontrollable proles walked the streets, the city had an unusual feel, over-uncold and over-exciteful. The rocket bombs crashed manytimeser, and sometimes doubleplusbig blasts, unnear and unknowed.

The new Unluv Song had been versifyed and was ever-played on telescreens: an animalful, sharp rhythm nearsame the hammering of a drum. Loudspeaked to the sound of marching foots, it was terrorful. The proles songed it, and in the PM streets it warred with the popular *It Was Only an Unhopeful Dream*. The Parsons youths ever-played it, AM-PM, overloud, on their trumpets.

Smith's post-worktime at Winful House was fuller. Squads of volunteers, organized by Parsons, were prepping the street for Unluv Week, making flags, painting posters, upping flags on roofs, and throwing wires over the street for streamers. Parsons was prideful that Winful House would have 400m of streamers and flags. He was energized and as joyful as a bird. The uncold and the hands-on work gived him a reason for rewearing pants and an open shirt. He was everywhere: pushing, pulling, knifing, hammering, prepping, upping everybody with joyful outspeaks, and outstreaming an unendful—but untrue—supply of strong joy.

A new poster was speedwise allover the city: unwords, only an overbig, animalful trooper, 3m or 4m high, marching with flatface and oversize boots, a machinegun at his hip. From whatever angle Smith watched the poster, the gun arrowed straight at him. The poster was on every blank wall, even outnumbering pictures of BB. The Party over-excited the proles, usualwise halfhearted about the war, to plusluv of Oceania. As tho together with the Unluv Week feelings, the rocket bombs were killing bigger numbers of persons. A bomb dropped on a crowded movie-house, another on a playground, youths were blasted to pieces. There were plusunjoyful demos, Goldstein statues were fired, 100s of the trooper posters were ripped down, and a number of freemarkets were robbed in the disorder; then a story flyed round that betrayers were controlling the rocket bombs, and some oldpersons, who were questioned as maybe outsiders, were killed and their house fired.

In the room over Charrington's market, when they was able to go there, Julia and Smith layed side-by-side on the bed underwindow—naked. The room was their ownlifeful world. When they comed, they would unwear their coveralls and sexcrime with sweating bodys, then sleep and unsleep, and resexcrime.

4, 5, 6—7 sexcrimes during month06. Smith had stopped his habit of all-day harddrinking. He unneeded it. He had growed unthinner, his leg was healthfuller, his AM coughing stopped. Life was OK, he unwanted to make faces at the telescreen or loudspeak unclean-words. Now they had an unwatched-place, nearwise ownlife together. It was important the room over the freemarket existed. To know it was there, untouched, was nearsame as being in it. The room was their world, a place from the past. Smith usualwise stopped to speak with Charrington for a few minutes on his way upstairs. The oldman sometimes, or never, goed outside, and otherwise had nearwise no other dealers in the market. He had a shadowful existence between the unbig unlightful market, and an unbigger kitchen where he prepped his meals and heared a doubleplusold music-machine with an oversize trumpet.

He was joyful to speak with a person, walking thru his unuseful things. With his long nose and unthin eyeglasses and unstraight shoulders in a blackcoat, he was nearsame a collecter, not a freemarketeer. With an underjoy he would finger this-or-that piece of waste—a bottle-stopper, the painted top of a breaked box, some baby's hair in a metal case—unwanting that Smith should deal it, only that he should watch it. To speak with him was nearsame hearing an outweared music-box. He had pulled from the corners of his memory pieces of disremembered songs. 'You maybe interested...' he would joyspeak, self-downful, whenever he had a new piece of a song. But he remembered only a few lines of any song.

Smith and Julia knowed—in a way, it was never out of their minds—that what was now happening was for unlongtime. Sometimes their future unlife was as touchable as the bed they layed on, and they coholded in unhopeful sexcrime, nearsame a malperson holding a final piece of joy when the clock is within 5 minutes of flashing. But there were also times when they daydreamed of ever-sexcrimes. In that room, they cofeeled, dishealth was unable to come to them. Going there was difficult and unsafe, but the room itself was an ownlifeful world. Nearsame the heart of the paperweigher, with Smith feeling it was possible to get inside that glass-world, where time would stop. Manytimes they uncrimestopped and daydreamed: their goodluck would stay forever, and they would do sexcrimes for all of their lifes. Or they would kill Katharine, and with shadowful moves they would marry. Or they would self-kill. Or they would self-vaporize: rectify themselfs unrecognizable, learn prolespeak, work in a factory and have unwatched lifestyles in a backstreet. It was all nonthink, they knowed. There wasn't an out. Even the plan that was doable, self-kill, they unplanned to do. Existing, day-to-day and week-to-week, a present without a future, was unstoppable animalthink, as lungs always inbreath air.

Sometimes, they speaked of doing antiParty crimes, but unknowed how to take step01. It was difficult to find their way into the shadowful Brotherhood. He speaked to her of the unusual cofeeling that existed, or maybe existed, with O'Brien, and how he sometimes wanted to speak to him about being an antiParty enemy and get his help. Julia unthinked this was a doubleplusuncareful thing to do. She habitwise watched person's facecrimes and understanded that Smith thinked O'Brien was politcrimeful, because of a single flash of the eyes.

But she unthinked that an outspread, organized counterRevolution existed or was able to exist. The storys about Goldstein and the underground enemy were a waste-pile. She had only the unlightfullest thinking about Goldstein. She was post-Revolution and overyouthful, disremembering the mind-wars of year50s and year60s. Politcrime was outside her thinking, and the Party was overpowerful. It would ever-exist, ever-same. Their antiParty crimes were sexcrimes, but they thinked of killing somebody or bombing something.

Otherwise, Julia speaked about 2minUnluv: it was doubleplusdifficult to unfacecrime, to crimestop outbursting in joyspeak. But she only questioned Party teachings when they touched her ownlife. Manytimes she was OK with Party news storys, because the change between true and untrue was unimportant to her. She thinked, for example, having learned it at school, the Party had invented airplanes, helicopters, and electric motors. And when he speaked to her about airplanes existing ante-Revolution, she thinked true/untrue was doubleplusuninteresting. Was it important who invented airplanes?

Plusshockful to him, he finded she disremembered that Oceania, 4 ante-years, had been unwarring. 'I think we've been at war forever,' she speaked, unclearwise. It was terrorful. He thinked, had the changeover happened 4 ante-years? He speaked with her about it for a quarter-hour. In the end, he overpowered her memory, but she thinked it was unimportant.

'Who cares?' she speaked, unpatienceful. 'It's always f'ckin' war, and the news is all untrue anyway.'

Sometimes he speaked about his important workpieces at Recdep and the whole process of rectifying records. Those things were unterrorful to her. She unfeeled the hole opening underfoot, as untrue becomed true.

'Every record has been vaporized or rectifyed, every book has been rewrited, every picture has been repainted, every statue and street and building has been renamed, every date has been updated, ever-processing, minute-by-minute and day-by-day, it's the end of history, nothing exists except the ever-present, the Party is ever-correct, I *know* the past is rectifyed, but it's unpossible for me to evidence it, and even when I rectifyed it, post-workpiece, there's unevidence, the only evidence is inside my own mind, inside my own mind, and I unknow anybody with the same memory...'

'...and what good is that?'

'It's ungood, but we're able to think of a counterRevolution, here-and-there, unbig groups of persons unspeedwise growing, and even leaving a few records, so the post-generation is able to start where we stopped.'

'I'm not interested in the post-generation, luv. I'm interested in *us*.'

'You're only an antiParty crimethinker from the waist down.'

She thinked his words were overjoyful and throwed her arms round him. But whenever he speaked about changing the past, and withholding the true, she becomed sleepful. Why worry about it? She knowed when to joyspeak and when to unjoyspeak, and that was all she needed. If he stayed on those subjects, she had an unnerving habit of sleeping. He thought she unwatched what was happening. By misunderstanding, she stayed sane.

chapter06

It had happened. The message had come. All his life, he had been waiting for this to happen.

He was walking down the long hallway at Minitrue, and he was near the place where Julia had handed him the message, when he felt that somebody bigger was walking behind him. The person, whoever it was, gived an unbig cough, ante-speaking. Smith stopped speedwise and turned. It was O'Brien.

Now, they were face-to-face, and his only feeling was to runaway. His heart jumped powerfulwise. He was unable to speak, but O'Brien layed an unenemyful hand on Smith's arm, and they were walking side-by-side. He started speaking with his serious style, unsame the majority of Inner Party members.

'I was hoping to speak with you. I was reading your report in *The Times*, doubleante-day. You have a teacher's interest in Dictionary words, I think?'

Smith had recovered some self-control. 'Unteacherful. It's not my subject. I never had anything to do with wording.'

'But you write plusbeautyful. That's not only my thinking. I was speaking to a coworker of yours who is a reworder. I unremember his name...'

Syme! Smith's heart moved unjoyfulwise. It was unthinkable this was anything otherwise a reference to Syme. But Syme was vaporized, an *unperson*. Referencing him was unsafe: self-vaporization. O'Brien's words must clearwise be a sign, a codeword. With an unbig act of crimethink he had changed them into cocrimers.

O'Brien stopped in front of the hallway telescreen. With his disarming joyful move, he reweared his eyeglasses. Then he respeaked:

'What I truewise wanted to speak to you about was your report. You used 2 unwords. But they're only now becoming unwords. Have you readed Dictionary number10?'

'No, I unthinked it had been published. We're using number09 in Recdep.'

'Number10 is unpublished for a few post-months, I think. But a few ante-copys have been outspreaded. It may interest you to read it, maybe?'

'Doubleplus,' speaked Smith, speedwise knowing where the conversation was going.

'Some of the new wording is doubleplusthinkful. The down-number of act-words—that will speak to you, I think. Will I send a messager to you with the Dictionary? But I always disremember anything of that type. Maybe you're able to get it at my house sometime? Wait. I'll give you my housenumber.'

They were standing in front of the telescreen. Semi-unmindful, O'Brien outpocketed an unbig notebook and gold pen. In front of the telescreen, where anybody watching was able to read it, he writed a housenumber, ripped out the page, and handed it to Smith.

'I'm usualwise there post-work. If not, my server will give you the Dictionary.'

He goed, leaving Smith holding the piece of paper which, this time, was unneeded to be unwatched. But he carefulwise remembered what was writed on it, and a few post-hours memory-holed it with other papers.

They had been cospeaking for a few minutes. The meet had been planned as a way to give him O'Brien's housenumber: 'If you ever want to contact me, this is where I am.' Maybe there would be a message somewhere in the Dictionary. But he knowed 100%: the counterRevolution, that he had dreamed of, existed, and he was at the outer edges of it.

He knowed that unlater-or-later he would follow O'Brien's message. Maybe post-day, maybe longer—he unknowed. What was happening was only the working-out of a process that had started 7 ante-years.
    step01 had been an unwatched, unvolunteerful think.
    step02 had been the opening of the daybook. He had moved from thinks to words, and now from words to acts.
    step03 was something that would happen in Miniluv.
He was OK with it. The end was within the start. But it was terrorful: it was nearsame a forecast of unlife, nearsame being minuslifeful. While speaking to O'Brien, when he understanded the meaning of the words, his body feeled cold, shaking, nearsame he was a skeleton underground, in a hole that he ever-knowed was waiting for him.

chapter07

Smith unsleeped with eyes full of tears. Julia rolled to him, sleepful, lowspeaking something. 'What's...'

'I dreamed...' he started, and stopped. It was overcomplex, unspeakable in words. There was the dream itself, and a memory connected to it, which swimmed into his mind in the milliseconds post-sleep.

He layed on his back with his eyes unopened, his mind full of the dreamful atmosphere. It was a plusbig, lightful dream, his whole life was in front of him, nearsame a landscape on a summer day post-rain. He was inside the glass paperweigher, but the glass was the sky, and the sky was full of clear soft light, and he was able to watch doubleplusunnear places. The dream was about his parent's arm-move, and that same move again, 30 post-years, by the woman he had watched in the movie, attempting to safeguard her youth from bullets, as the helicopter gunned them both to pieces.

'Do you know,' he questioned 'I thinked I killed my parent?'

'Why did you kill her?' questioned Julia, nearwise sleeping.

In the dream, he remembered the final time with his parent, and within a few post-seconds of unsleeping, the group of unbig events had all returned. It was a memory he had disremembered, blackwhiteful. He unknowed the date, but he was maybe age10 or age12.

He remembered the overloud, worryful time: terrorful airwars, safeguarding in Tube stations, piles of breaked stones everywhere, unreadable posters on street corners, youth groups in white shirts, overlong lines outside feed markets, on-and-off machinegun sounds unnear—overall, he remembered, there was never enough feed: long days with other youths tracking thru waste-piles, getting leafs, potatos, or breadcrusts from which they carefulwise cleaned the dust; waiting for trucks carrying cowfeed, which sometimes dropped feed when they goed over the malrepaired streets.

When 1 of Smith's parents was vaporized, his other parent unshowed any shock or any powerful unjoy, but she speedwise changed. She becomed doubleplusunspirited. It was clear even to Smith that she was waiting for something that she knowed must happen. She did everything—cooked, cleaned, maked repairs, maked the bed, cleaned the floor, dusted the overshelf—always plusunspeedwise and overcareful, nearsame an auto-doll. Her big shapeful body stopped for hours; she sitted nearwise unmoving on the bed, holding his youthful sister, a doubleplusunbig, unhealthful, unspeaking girl of age02 or age03, with a face thinned and maked nearsame a monkey from overhunger.

Sometimes she holded Smith in her arms and pressed him to her for longtime, unspeaking. He knowed, tho he was youthful and ownlifeful, that her acts connected to the unspeaked thing that was near happening.

He remembered the room they inhabited, an unlightful, ungood-smelling room that was half-full of a bed with white bedcover. There was a gas-stove at the fireplace, and a feedshelf, and a brown sink in the hallway, used by all cohabiters. He remembered his parent's beautyful body unstraightening over the gas-stove to mix something in a cookpot. Overall, he remembered his ever-hunger, and the overpowerful, warring arguments at mealtimes. He ever-questioned his parent, over-and-over-and-over, why he was unfeeded. He loudspeaked at her, or he attempted to make her unjoyfuller to get feed. His parent feeded him. She thinked he needed the biggest parts of the meals; but he always loudspeaked for bigger parts. Every mealtime she speaked to him, down-feeling and underful, to be unownlifeful and remember that his unbig sister was unhealthful and also needed feed, but it was unuseful. He loudspeaked with unjoy when she stopped spooning, attempted to pull the cookpot and spoon out of her hands, and taked feed from his sister's bowl. He knowed he was overhungering his parent and sister, but he was unable to crimestop; he feeled that the feed was his. A loud hunger in his belly, between mealtimes. If his parent unsafeguarded it, he robbed the feedshelf.

He remembered plusclearwise an unbig piece of chocolate, unrationed ante-weeks or -months, to be knifed into 3 same-size parts. Speedwise, as tho hearing somebody else, Smith heared himself loudspeaking that he wanted the whole piece. His parent speaked to him, 'Don't be ownlifeful,' and longtime arguing that goed round-and-round, with loudspeaking, counter-arguing, unjoyspeaking, counter-speaking. His unbig baby sister, holding onto her parent with both hands, watched him with big, unjoyful eyes. In the end, his parent breaked off 3/4 of the chocolate and gived it to Smith, giving the other 1/4 to his sister, who holded it, maybe unknowing what it was. Smith watched her for a second. With a speedful jump he pulled the piece of chocolate from his sister's hand and was running to the door.

'Stop!' his parent loudspeaked. 'Give your sister her chocolate!'

He stopped, but unreturned. His parent's worryful eyes were watching his face. His sister, knowing that she had been robbed of something, started an unstrong unjoyspeak. His parent placed her arm round her baby and pressed her face to her breast. Something in the move speaked to him: his sister had unlifeful dishealth.

He turned and downstaired, with the chocolate in his hand. He never rewatched his parent.

Post-robbing the chocolate, he feeled shameful and stayed in the street for a few hours, then hunger maked him return. His parent had vaporized. This was becoming usual at that time. Nothing was outed from the room, except his parent and his sister. They hadn't taked any wears, not even his parent's overcoat. Today, he ever-unknowed if his parent was unlifeful. It was possible she had goed to joycamp with his sister, or his sister maybe goed to Reclaimcen, same as Smith.

The dream was clear in his mind, doubleplusclear was the rounding, safeguardful arm-move, which holded the dream's whole meaning. His mind returned to that other dream, 2 ante-months: his parent sitted on the unclean white bedcover, with the baby holding onto her, samewise she had sitted in the boat, plusunder him, down deeper every minute, but upwatching him thru the unlightening water.

He speaked to Julia about the story of his parent vaporizing. Unopening her eyes, she rolled over and repositioned herself gooder.

'I think you were an unbig pig in those days,' she speaked, unclear. 'All youths are pigs.'

'Yes. But the story is...' From her breathing it was clear that she was resleeping. He wanted to speak about his parent. He thinked, from what he was able to remember, that she had been an unthinkful woman. Smith robbed the chocolate, and she holded the baby in her arms. It was unuseful, it changed nothing, it unproduced chocolate, it unchanged the baby's life or her ownlife. The outsider woman in the boat had also covered her unbig youth with her arm, which unsafeguarded him from the bullets. The proles, he speedwise crimethinked, were untrueheartful to the Party or Airfield01, they were trueheartful only to other proles. It was time01 in his lifetime that he luved the proles. They had heart and animalthink. And he remembered a few ante-weeks, he had kicked a knifed hand into the street, as tho it was waste.

He thinked for an unlongtime. 'Have you ever thinked,' he questioned, 'that the goodest thing for us is to walkout of here and never remeet?'

'Yes, luv, I thinked it, a few times. But I'm undoing it, all the same.'

'We've been goodluckful, but we're unable to stay goodluckful. You're doubleplusyouthful. You're usual and unshameful. If you stay away from persons nearsame me, you maybe lifeful for 50 post-years.'

'No. I've thinked it all out. What you do, I'm going to do. And don't be overdownhearted. I'm plusgood at staying lifeful.'

'We maybe together for 6 post-months, 1 post-year. Who knows? At the end we'll be disconnected. Do you understand how single we'll be? When they stop us, there'll be nothing, nothing, that we're able to do for each other. Nothing that I'm able to do or speak. We'll be 100% unpowerful. The importantest thing is that we unbetray each other.'

'If you mean answering questions, we'll do that, 100%. Everybody always answers. You're unable to stop it. They question you.'

'I don't mean answering questions. Answers don't betray. What you speak or do is unimportant: only your heart is important. If they're able to make me stop luving you—that would be truewise betraying you.'

She thinked about it. 'They're unable to do that. It's the 1 thing they're unable to do. They'll make you speak anything—*anything*—but they're unable to make you think it. They're unable to get inside you.'

'No,' he speaked, hopefuller. 'No, that's 100% true. They're unable to get inside you. If you're able to *feel* that staying human is important, even without any outcome, then you've overthrowed them.'

He thinked of the telescreen with its never-sleeping eyes and ears. They were able to spy on him AM-PM, but if he was thinkful he was able to outthink them. With all their overthinking, they had never invented a way to hear what another person was thinking. But maybe that was untrue when a person was inside Miniluv: drugs, careful machines that recorded nerve reacts, unspeedful pushing-down by unsleep and over-single, AM-PM ever-questioning. His inner mind was finded, tracked down by questions; outed. But if he unwanted to stay lifeful, but only to stay human, his inner mind was unimportant. They were unable to rectify his heart: he was unable to self-rectify it, even if he wanted to. They were able to expose everything he had done or speaked or thinked; but his inner heart, whose workings were self-unwatched, was unbreakable.

chapter08

They had done it, they had done it!

They were standing in a long-shaped and unlightful room. The telescreen was downlighted; the deep, plusblue carpet was nearsame walking on grass. At the room-end O'Brien was sitting at a table under a greenlight, with a pile of papers on bothsides. He hadn't upwatched when his server bringed in Julia and Smith.

Smith's heart was drumming so speedwise that he questioned if he was able to speak. They had done it, they had done it, was all he was able to think. It had been an underthinkful act to come here together; tho they had come by unsame routes and meeted on O'Brien's doorstep. It was only sometimes that he watched Inner Party houses, or comed into this district. The whole atmosphere of the doubleplusbig houses, the money and over-space of everything, the unknowed smells of good feed, the unsoundful and plusspeedful uppers, upping-and-downing, the whitecoat servers speeding here-and-there—everything was over him. Tho he had a good reason for coming here, he was shadowed at every step by the terror that a black-uniform safeguard would speedwise round the corner, overwatch his ID, and order him to out.

O'Brien's server had inned them unspeakful. He was an unbig man in whitecoat, with an angled doubleplusflatface. He leaded them down a hallway with a carpet and white walls, all 100% clean. That also was over him; Smith unknowed hallways with walls untouched by bodys.

O'Brien had a piece of paper between his fingers and was reading it, serious. His heavy face was both terrorful and knowing. For maybe 20 seconds he sitted unmoving. Then he pulled the speakwrite to him and speakwrited a message:

'Start message number01, -05, -07 OKed fullwise stop number06 doubleplusunthinkful nearwise crimethink undo stop ungo buildwise ante-getting plusfull numbers machine overheads stop end message.'

He upped unspeedwise from his chair and comed to them over the unsoundful carpet. The Party atmosphere had dropped away from him, but he was flatface, as tho unjoyful to stop working. Smith feeled terrorful, and now also shameful. It was pluspossible he had misthinked. What evidence had he that O'Brien was a counterRevolution politcrimer? Only a flash of the eyes and a single unclear message: only his own dreams and daydreams. He was unable to mask that he had come for the Dictionary, because Julia was also here. O'Brien turned and pressed a button on the wall. There was a sharp click. The telescreen offed.

Julia speaked a doubleplusunbig sound of shock. Even mid-terror, Smith was also over-shocked, unable to stop his tongue.

'You're able to off it!'

'Yes, we're able to off it,' speaked O'Brien.

He was opposite them now. His solid body towered over them, and his face was unreadable. He was waiting, semi-serious, for Smith to speak, but about what? Even now it was pluspossible that he was an overworked man questioning, unjoyful, why he had been workstopped. Nobody speaked. Off-telescreen, the room was terrorwise unsoundful. The seconds were oversize. Smith stayed watching O'Brien's eyes, but it was difficult. Then speedwise the flatface changed into maybe a joyface. With his usual move, O'Brien reweared his eyeglasses.

'Do I speak, or will you?' he questioned.

'I'll speak. That thing's truewise off?'

'Yes, everything is off. We're ownlife.'

'We've come here because...'

He stopped, knowing that his reasons were unclear. Because he unknowed what help he wanted from O'Brien, it was difficult to speak about why they'd come here. He respeaked, knowing that what he was speaking sounded both unstrong and overfull:

'We think there's a counterRevolution, some unwatched organization working antiParty, and that you're part of it. We want to join it and work for it. We're enemys of the Party. We disthink the Orders of Party. We're crimethinkers. We're also sexcrimers. I speak about this because we want to place ourselfs under your control. If you want us to self-betray otherwise, we're prepped to do that.'

He stopped and speedwise sidewatched, feeling that the door had opened. 100% true, the unbig server had inned, unknocking. Smith watched him carrying a tray with a bottle and glasses.

'Martin is 1 of us,' speaked O'Brien, flatface. 'Bring the drinks here, Martin. Place them on the round table. Have we enough chairs? Then sit down and speak. Bring a chair for yourself, Martin. This is work. Stop being a server for 10 minutes.'

The unbig man sitted down, plusjoyful, but ever-serverful. Smith watched him out of the corner of his eye. The man's whole life was a mask, and he feeled it unsafe to drop his mask even for a second. O'Brien taked the bottle by the neck and fulled the glasses with a plusred liquid. Overwatched, the stuff was nearwise black, but in the bottle it flashed red. It had an unsweet-sweet smell. He watched Julia up her glass and smell it with true interest.

'It's a type of harddrink,' speaked O'Brien with an unbig joyface. 'It ungoes to the Outer Party...' His face was reserious, and he upped his glass: 'I think it's plusgood that we start by drinking to the health of our leader: Goldstein.'

Smith upped his glass, truewise heartful, but when he drinked it, the stuff was plusdisheartening—not his type of harddrink. He downed the unfull glass.

'There *is* a person named Goldstein?' he questioned.

'Yes, there is, but I don't know where.'

'And the counterRevolution—the organization? Is it true? Or is it an invention of Thinkpol?'

'Yes, the Brotherhood, we call it. You'll unlearn info about the Brotherhood, but it exists, and you're part of it. I'll return to that later.' He watched the clock. 'It's unthinkful, even for Inner Party members, to be off-telescreen for over half-hour. You shouldn't have come here together, and you must leave otherwise. You,'—he downed his head to Julia—'will ante-leave. We have about 20 minutes. You understand that I must start with some questions. What are you prepped to do?'

'Anything that we're able to,' speaked Smith.

O'Brien turned in his chair so that he was facing Smith. He nearwise diswatched Julia, thinking that Smith was able to speak for her. He speedwise unopened his eyes. He started questioning in a low, unfeeling speak, as tho this was the usual series and he knowed the answers.

'You're prepped to give your lifes?'

'Yes'

'You're prepped to kill?'

'Yes'

'To workstop, which maybe kills 100s of persons?'

'Yes'

'Betray the Party to outside powers?'

'Yes'

'You're prepped to be ever-untrue, to self-print money, to turn youthful minds unlawful, to push drugs, to deal sexcrimes, to outspread dishealthful sex—to do everything to disenpower the Party?'

'Yes'

'Throw acid in a baby's face—are you prepped to do that?'

'Yes'

'You're prepped to undo your ID and be a server or factory-worker for your lifetime?'

'Yes'

'You're prepped to self-kill, if and when we order you to do so?'

'Yes'

'You're prepped, the 2 of you, to disconnect and never remeet?'

'No!' loudspeaked Julia.

Smith taked a longtime ante-answer. He was unable to speak. His tongue worked, unsoundful, making the opening of a word, then another word, over-and-over-and-over. He unknowed which word he was going to speak.

Then he speaked. 'No.'

'It was good to speak true to me. We need to know everything.'

He turned to Julia and speaked, semi-feelful:

'Do you understand that even if he's lifeful, it maybe as an unsame person? We maybe give him a new ID. His face, his moves, the shape of his hands, his hair color—even his speak will be unsame. And you maybe an unsame person. We're able to rectify persons unrecognizable. Sometimes it's needed. Sometimes we even knife off arms-or-legs.'

Smith speedwise sidewatched Martin's face. Unscarred, he thinked. Julia's face turned lighter, but she faced O'Brien: strong, heartful, spirited. She lowspeaked something, maybe 'yes.'

'Good. Then that's answered.'

Blank-mindful, O'Brien standed and started to walk unspeedwise, as tho he thinked gooder standing. He rewatched the clock.

'You should return to the kitchen, Martin. I'll on the telescreen in a quarter-hour. Remember these faces. You'll rewatch them. I'll maybe not.'

Same as he did at the frontdoor, Martin's eyes flashed over their faces. There wasn't any joy in his face. He was remembering their faces, but he was uninterested in them. Smith thought that his face was maybe solid, unable to change. Unspeaking, Martin outed, unopening the door behind him. O'Brien was walking up-down, a hand inpocketed his black coveralls.

'You understand that you'll be warring in the unlight. You'll always be in the unlight. You'll get orders and you'll follow them, unknowing why. Later I'll send you *the book* from which you'll learn about the true of our society, and the plans to break it. When you have readed *the book*, you'll be full members of the Brotherhood. But between the end that we're warring for and the present work, you'll unknow anything. The Brotherhood exists, but I'm unable to speak about the numbers, maybe 100 members or maybe 10,000,000. From your personal knowledge, you'll be unable to speak about numbers over 12. You'll have 3 or 4 contacts, who will be renewed time-to-time as they vaporize. As I'm your contact, you'll get orders from me. If we need to speak with you, it'll be thru Martin. When you're catched, you'll answer questions. That's unavoidable. But you'll have few answers, otherwise your own acts. You'll betray only a handful of unimportant persons. Maybe you won't even be able to betray me. By that time I maybe unlifeful, or I'll have become an unsame person, with an unsame face.'

He ever-moved, here-and-there, over the soft carpet. Tho big in body, his moves were plusgood, smooth, even the move of inpocketing his hands. Powerful, self-true, with a semi-blackwhiteful understanding of goodthink; he wasn't single-minded. When he speaked of killing, self-killing, dishealthful sex, knifed arms-or-legs, and rectifyed faces, it was nearsame blackwhite.

A type of luv, nearwise worship, outstreamed from Smith to O'Brien. He had disremembered the shadowful Goldstein. When he watched O'Brien's powerful shoulders and his unsharp face, unbeautyful but civilized, it was unpossible to think he was able to be overpowered. He knowed all plans, ante-watched all. Julia also feeled it; she was watching him, serious. O'Brien respeaked:

'You've heared storys of the Brotherhood. You have your own picture of it. You think, maybe, it's a doubleplusbig underworld of counterRevolutioners, unwatched, meeting underground, writing messages on walls, recognizing each other by codewords or by unusual hand-moves. Nothing of the type exists. Brotherhood members are unable to recognize each other, and every member knows the ID of only a few others. Goldstein, if he was in the hands of Thinkpol, would be unable to give them a member list, or any info that would lead them to a list. No list exists. The Brotherhood won't be cleaned up because it's an unusual organization. Nothing togethers it except groupthink, which is unbreakable. You'll never have anything to support you, except that groupthink. When you're catched, you'll be unhelped. We never help our members. When it's needed that somebody should be unspeakful, we're sometimes able to get a razor into a prisoner's room. You must become habitful of life without outcomes and without hope. You'll work, you'll be catched, you'll answer their questions, and then you'll be unlifeful. Those are the only outcomes that you'll ever know. It's unpossible any true change will happen within our ownlifetimes. We're the unlifeful. Our only true life is in the future. We'll take part in it as handfuls of dust and pieces of bone. But the future is unknowable. It maybe 1,000 post-years. We're unable to act together. We're only able to outspread our knowledge person-to-person, generation-to-generation. In the face of Thinkpol there isn't another way.'

He stopped and watched the clock.

'It's near time for you to leave,' he speaked to Julia. 'Wait. The bottle's half-full.'

He fulled the glasses and upped his glass.

'What will it be this time?' He speaked with the same unbig blackwhite. 'To crimes antiThinkpol? To unlife of BB? To all humans? To the future?'

'To the past,' speaked Smith.

'The past is importanter,' O'Brien speaked, serious.

They unfulled their glasses, and Julia standed to go. O'Brien taked an unbig cube from the overshelf and handed her a white tablet to place on her tongue. It was important, he speaked, to unsmell of harddrink: the upper servers were pluswatchful. When the door unopened behind her, he disremembered her existence. He walked, up-down, then stopped.

'There are somethings to be answered. You have an unwatched-place of some type?'

Smith speaked about the room over Charrington's freemarket.

'That's good for now. Later, we'll plan something else for you. It's important to change your unwatched-place sometimes. Until then, I'll send you a copy of *the book*—Goldstein's book—when it's possible. It maybe some post-days. There aren't many in existence. Thinkpol tracks them down and vaporizes them, nearwise as speedful as we're able to produce them, but *the book* is unbreakable. If the final copy is vaporized, we're able to reproduce it nearwise word-for-word. Do you carry a workcase with you?'

'Yes'

'What is it?'

'Black, plusoutweared. With 2 straps.'

'Black, 2 straps, plusoutweared—good. Someday in the near future—I'm unable to give you the date—one of your work messages will have a misprinted word, and you'll order a reprint. On the post-day you'll go to work without your workcase. Sometime during the day, in the street, a man will touch you on the arm and speak "I think you've dropped your workcase." The 1 he gives you will have a copy of Goldstein's book. You'll return it within 14 post-days.'

They were unspeakful for a second.

'There are a few minutes ante-leaving. We'll remeet—if we do remeet...'

Smith upwatched him. '...in the place where there's no unlight?' he speaked, semi-stopful.

O'Brien updowned, unshocked. 'In the place where there's no unlight,' he respeaked, as tho he recognized the reference. 'And now, it's time for you to go. But wait. I'll give you a tablet.'

As Smith standed O'Brien outed a hand. His powerful hold nearwise breaked Smith's hand-bones. At the door, Smith rewatched O'Brien, but he was in the process of disremembering him, doublethinkful. He was waiting, with his finger on the telescreen control-button, the writing-table behind him, with greenlight and speakwrite and holders overfull of papers. The event was unopened. Within 30 post-seconds, he thought, O'Brien would return to his important Party work.

chapter09

Smith was gelful. *Gelful* was the correct word. It comed into his head speedwise. His body was as unstrong and clear as gel. He feeled that if he upped his hand he would be able to watch sunlight thru it. All lifeblood and energy had outstreamed from him by overwork, leaving only an unstrong body of nerves, bones, and skin. All his feelings were bigger: his coveralls down-pressed his shoulders, the street unjoyed his foots, opening and unopening his hand maked finger-sounds.

He had overworked 90 hours in 5 days. Everybody in Minitrue had overworked. Now it was allover, and he had nothing to do, no Party work of any type, post-day. He would be able to stay 6 hours in their unwatched-place, and another 9 in his own bed. Unspeedwise, in unstrong sun, he walked up an unclean street to Charrington's market, semi-watchful for Thinkpol, but nonthinkful, thinking this day he was unwatched and nobody was spying on him. The heavy workcase banged his knee at each step, flashing an electric feeling up-down the skin of his leg. Inside was *the book*, which he'd had for 6 ante-days and yet unopened.

Unluv Week: parades, loudspeaks, songs, flags, posters, movies, statues, drums hammering and trumpets blasting, the sound of marching foots, the grinding of war machines, the oversound of warplanes, guns blasting. On day06, the doubleplusbig climax was bodyful shaking to its climax, and everybody's unluv was overfired, plusdreamful. If the crowd was able to handle the 2,000 warcrimers, who were to be executed in public on the final day, they would have, unquestioning, ripped them to pieces—Oceania was at war!

Smith was in a PM demo at the Square. The whitefaces and the red flags were over-lighted. The Square was packed with 10,000s of persons, with a youthful crowd of about 1,000 Spys. In front of a red background, an Inner Party speaker, a thin man with overlong arms and a big naked skull with few hairs, was broadsiding the crowd. An unbig person, misshaped by unluv, he holded the mic neck while his other hand, oversize at the end of a bone-thin arm, ripped at the air overhead, threatful. His loudspeaking, upped and metalful, blasted out a long list of warcrimes: group-killings, robbings, rapes, questioning of prisoners, bombings of citys, untrue news.

It was near unpossible to hear him and unthink warcrimes were evidenced and then unfeel disjoy. Every few seconds the unjoy of the crowd overfired and the loudspeaker was overpowered by an animal sound that outburst, uncontrolled, from 1,000s of throats. The animalest loudspeaks comed from the Spy youths.

The speaker, holding the mic, his shoulders rounded, his other hand ripping at the air, was ever-speaking. The animal oversounds of unluv were blasting from the crowd, ever-unluvful. A blankface man touched him on the shoulder and speaked: 'I think you dropped your workcase.'

He taked the workcase, unthinking and unspeaking. He knowed it would be a few post-days when he had time to read it. The millisecond the demo ended, he goed straight to Minitrue, tho it was near 23:00. All Minitrue workers did samewise. The telescreen orders about overtime were unneeded.

Oceania was at war: Oceania had forever been at war. Reports and records of all types, newspapers, books, booklets, movies, soundtracks, photos—all must be rectifyed at light-speed. Unordered but all-knowed, Recdep heads planned that post-week all references would unexist anywhere. The overwork was unable to be called by its true name. Everybody in Recdep worked overtime, 18 hours in 24, with 3-hour sleep breaks. Mattresses were upped from sublevels and layed allover the hallways: servers bringed meals of sandwichs and coffee from the cafe. Everytime Smith taked a sleep break, he attempted to leave his desk clear of work, and everytime he returned, sleep- eyed and unenergyful, he finded paper tubes covering the desk, half-undering the speakwrite and overstreaming onto the floor, so his ante-work was always to place them in an orderful pile to give himself a workspace. The work was difficult and not 100% machineful. Manytimes it was OK to replace and rename, but any stat report of events needed careful rethinking, using his knowledge of maps and the war.

By day03 his eyes over-disjoyed and his eyeglasses needed cleaning every few minutes. It was nearsame warring with some difficult workpiece, something which he was able to stop doing, but which he was nerveful worryed to do 100% correct. When he had time to remember it, he worryed that every word he lowspeaked into the speakwrite, every word from his pen, should be thinkful. He was as worryed as anybody else in Recdep that the news should be 100% correct. AM day06, the stream from the newtubes downspeeded. For a half-hour, nothing outed the newtube; then 1; then nothing. Everywhere, about sametime, the work was stopping. A deep outbreath goed thru Recdep. Doubleplusoverwork, which would never be speaked about, had been done. It was now possible for anybody to evidence, by docful evidence, that the war had happened. At 12:00 it was broadcasted that all Minitrue workers were offwork until AM post-day. Smith, carrying his workcase, *the book* within, which had stayed between his foots while he worked and under his body while he sleeped, returned to Winful House, razored, and nearwise sleeped in his bath, tho the water was under-uncold.

With a type of joyful sound in his bones, he upped the stairs over Charrington's market. He was unenergyful, but unsleepful. He opened the window, and placed a coffeepot on the unclean unbig oilstove. Julia would come; until then, there was *the book*. He sitted in the unclean armchair and unstrapped the workcase.

A heavy black book, disordered and malprinted, unnamed on the cover. The print was also unusual. The page-edges were outweared and ripped, as tho the book had been touched by many hands.

Somewhere doubleplusunnear a rocket bomb crashed down. The joyful feeling of being ownlife with the outlaw book, in a room untelescreened. His unenergyful body in the soft chair, the unstrong wind thru the window touched his cheek. Unsound except the clicking of the clock. The book plusinterested him. It was the product of an unsane mind nearsame his own. The goodest books, he knowed, are those that speaked about what he ante-knowed.

He heared Julia's footstep on the stairs and outed his chair to meet her. She dropped her brown toolbox on the floor and throwed herself into his arms.

'I have *the book*,' he speaked, as they distogethered themselfs.

'O, you have it? Good,' she speaked, uninterested, and speedwise downed beside the oilstove to make coffee.

They unreturned to the subject until they had sexcrimed in bed for a half-hour. The PM weather was semi-cold; they pulled up the bedcover. From the street comed the ante-heared sounds of songs and boots on the stones. The woman with muscleful red arms was nearwise always in the backyard. There maybe no hour of daylight when she wasn't marching between the cleaning-sink and the line, mouth full of wearclips and joyful song. Julia was laying on her side and near-sleeping. He upped *the book*, which was laying on the floor, and upsitted.

'We must read it. You also. All Brotherhood members must read it.'

'You read it,' she speaked, with her eyes unopened. 'Read it. That's the goodest way. Then we'll speak about it.'

The clock hands showed 6:00, meaning 18:00. They had 3 or 4 post- hours. He placed *the book* on his knees and started reading out-loud.

'Julia, are you unsleep?'

'Yes, my luv, I hear you. Go on. It's doubleplusgood.'

Post-sometime, Smith heared the unsound, same as hearing a new sound. He thinked that Julia was plusunmoving. She was laying on her side, naked from the waist up, with her cheek pillowed on her hand and blackhair over her eyes. Her breasts upped-and-downed, unspeedwise and timewise.

'Julia'

No answer.

'Julia, are you unsleep?'

No answer. She was sleeping. He unopened *the book*, placed it carefulwise on the floor, layed down, and pulled the bedcover over both of them.

He had, he thinked, unlearned the final answer from *the book*. He understanded *how*; he disunderstanded *why*. *The book* unspeaked about anything that he unknowed; it had only systematized his ante-knowledge. Post-reading, he knowed that he was in a minority, a minority of 1, but he stayed thinking the whole world was unsane.

Yellow light from the downing sun angled thru the window and onto the pillow. He unopened his eyes. The sun on his face and the girl's smooth body touching his own gived him a strong, sleepful, self-true feeling. He was unwatched; everything was OK. He sleeped lowspeaking 'Sane isn't stats,' feeling those words holded plusdeep thinks.

chapter10

When he unsleeped, it was with the feeling of having slept for a longtime, but he speedwise watched the clock, and it was only 20:30. He layed sleeping for sometime; then the usual deep-lunged song started from the backyard:

'It was only an 'nopeful dream on a m'nth'4 dye
But a lo'k an' a word an' the dreams they moved
They 'ave tak'd my 'eart awye!'

The song was popular. He heared it allover the place. It was outlifefuller than the Unluv Song. Julia unsleeped at the sound, moved joyfulwise, and outed the bed.

'I'm hungerful. Let's make some coffee. F'ck! The stove's off and the water's cold.' She upped the stove and shaked it. 'There's no oil in it.'

'We'll get some from Charrington.'

'The unusual thing is, it was 100% full. I'm going to rewear my coveralls,' she plussed. 'It's colder.'

Smith also upped and weared his coveralls. The ever-energyful woman songed:

'They spe'k that time repai's all things,
They spe'k you're able t' always disrememb'r;
But the joys' an' the tears 'cross the years
They play with my 'eart forever!'

As he clipped the waist-strap of his coveralls, he walked to the window. The sun had downed behind the houses; it wasn't sunlighting the backyard. The streets were wet, as tho they had been cleaned, and he feeled the sky had been cleaned also, so new and uncolorful was the blue between the houses. Unending, the woman marched here-and-there, fulling and unfulling her mouth with wearclips, songing and then unsonging, and wearclipping, plus-and-plus.

Julia comed to his side; they downwatched the strong woman with plusinterest: her strong arms holding the line. Her powerful body, he thinked, was beautyful. He had never thinked the body of a woman age50, overbig and hard from work, was able to be beautyful. But it was and, he thinked, why not?

'She's beautyful,' he lowspeaked.

'She's over-broad at the hips.'

'That's her style of beauty.'

He rounded Julia's soft waist, undifficultwise, with his arm. Out of their bodys no baby would ever come. That was 1 thing they were unable to do. Only by word of mouth, mind-to-mind, were they able to move the counterRevolution into the future. The woman down there was unmindful, she had only strong arms, an uncold heart, and a healthful belly. He thinked how many babys she had. It maybe 15. She had her speedful flowering, a year, maybe, of youthful beauty and then she had speedwise growed big and hard and red and unsmooth, and then her life had been cleaning, repairing, cooking, repairing, cleaning, cooking for 30 years. At the end of it, she was songing. The otherworldful worship he feeled for her was complex, mixed with the uncolorful blue sky, outspeading over the cityscape.

It was unusual to think the sky was the same for everybody. And the persons under-sky were also nearsame—everywhere, allover the world, 100s,

1,000s, 1,000,000s of persons same as this woman, unknowing each other existed, parted by walls unluvful and untrue, but nearwise the same—persons who had never learned to think, but who had in their hearts and bellys and muscles the power that would someday overturn the world.

If there was hope, it was the proles! He had unreaded the end of *the book*, but he knowed that was Goldstein's final unsane message. The future was for the proles. And when their time comed, wouldn't the world they builded be as unsane to him, 6079 Smith, as the world of the Party? Yes, because it would be an unsane world. Where proles are on the same level as Party members, the world is unsane. The proles were everlifeful, he was unable to question it, when he watched the strong-heartful woman in the backyard. In the end their unsleeping would come. And ante-unsleep, tho it maybe 1,000 post-years, they would stay lifeful and goodluckful, nearsame birds, giving life body-to-body.

'Do you remember,' he questioned, 'the bird that songed to us, day01, at the woods-edge?'

'She wasn't songing to us. She enjoyed songing for herself. Not even that. She was only songing.'

The birds songed, the proles songed. All-round the world, in the unwatched outlaw lands, outside the frontline, in the streets of big citys, unbig citys, freemarkets—everywhere standed the same solid unstoppable woman, overbig from working her whole life, and ever-songful.

'We're unlifeful,' Smith speaked.

'We're unlifeful,' respeaked Julia, dutyful.

'You're unlifeful,' loudspeaked a metal sound behind them.

They jumped away. Smith's belly turned to ice. Julia's eyes were plusopen and white all-round. Her face turned white-yellow. The red paint on her cheekbones outstanded clear, as tho unconnected to her skin.

'You're unlifeful,' respeaked the metal sound.

'It was behind the picture,' breathed Julia.

'It was behind the picture,' it respeaked. 'Stay where you are. Unmove until you are ordered.'

It was starting, it was starting! They were only able to stand, watching each other's eyes. To run for life, to leave the house—they never thinked of that. Unthinkable to unfollow the loudspeaker in the wall. There was a click and a crash of breaking glass. The picture had dropped to the floor, uncovering the telescreen behind it.

'Now they're able to watch us,' speaked Julia.

'Now we're able to watch you. Stand mid-room. Stand back-to-back. Hands behind your heads. Untouch each other.'

They were untouching, but he was able to feel Julia's body shaking. Or maybe it was only the shaking of his own body. He was able to stop his tooths from clicking, but his knees were out-of-control. There was a sound of boots, inside-and-outside the house. The backyard full of mans. Something was pulled over the stones. The woman's song stopped speedwise.

'The house is all-rounded,' speaked Smith.

'The house is all-rounded,' respeaked the telescreen.

He heared Julia click her tooths together. She speaked 'Goodbye, luv.'

'Goodbye, luv,' the telescreen respeaked.

And then another sound, a teacherful speaker which Smith thinked he had ante-heared. 'And otherwise, while we're on the subject, "Here comes a candle to light you to bed, here comes a knifer to knife off your head!" '

Something crashed onto the bed behind Smith's back. They'd pushed thru the window and had inbursted the frame. Somebody was coming thru the window. The sound of boots upstairing, and the room was full of solid mans in black uniforms, with metal boots on their foots and clubs in their hands.

Smith was unshaking. He unmoved his eyes. 1 thing was important: stay unmoving! A flatface man, his mouth only a slit, stopped opposite Smith, thinkful, holding his club in his hand. Smith meeted his eyes, with his hands behind his head and his facecrime exposed. The man outed his white tongue, moved it round his thin lips, and then walked on. Another crash. Somebody had upped the glass paperweigher from the table and hammered it to pieces on the stove.

The piece of ocean-flower, a doubleplusunbig light-red folding, nearsame a sugar-flower, rolled over the carpet. How unbig, thinked Smith, how unbig it always was!

The mans upped Julia by her knees and shoulders, and carried her out of the room. Smith watched her, upsidedown, yellow and misshaped, with her eyes unopened, and red paint on her cheeks; and he unrewatched her.

He standed unmoving as an unlifeful skeleton. Doubleplusuninteresting thinks auto-started to speedwise move thru his mind. He thinked if they had stopped Charrington. He thinked what they had done to the woman in the backyard. He wanted to go to the toilet. He watched the clock on the overshelf; it showed 9:00, meaning 21:00. But the light was overstrong. Wouldn't the light be downing at 21:00 in month08? Had he and Julia misthinked the time—they oversleeped and thinked it was 20:30 when truewise it was 8:30 post-day? But he stopped thinking about it. It was uninteresting.

There was another, unlouder step in the hallway. Charrington comed into the room. The black-uniform mans speedwise becomed dutyful. Something had changed in Charrington. He eyed the pieces of the glass paperweigher.

'Get those pieces,' he speaked sharpwise.

A man downed to follow his order. The prolespeak had vaporized; Smith speedwise knowed he had been loudspeaking a few ante-seconds on the telescreen. Charrington was wearing his old blackcoat, but his hair, which had been near-white, was black, and he was unwearing eyeglasses. He gived Smith a single sharp speedwise eye, as tho verifying his ID, and then gived him unattention. Charrington was recognizable, but he was unsame. His body had straightened and growed bigger. His face had undergoed only doubleplusunbig changes, but it was 100% changeover. The black eyebrows were minusbushful, the face unlined, the nose unlonger, the whole face rectifyed. It was the watchful flatface of a man age35. Smith thinked it was time01 in his lifetime that he was watching, with knowledge, an undercover member of Thinkpol.

part03

chapter01

He unknowed where he was. Maybe he was in Miniluv, but there was noway of knowing. He was in a high-ceiling unwindowful room with mirror-white walls. Watchful lights fulled the room with cold light, and there was a low machine ever-sound, which he thinked had something to do with the air supply. A bench, or shelf broad enough to sit on, all-round the walls, the door, and at the opposite end a toilet. There were 4 telescreens, 1 in each wall.

There was an unsharp aching in his belly. Post-stop—they had throwed him in a truck and taked him away—he had ungood bellyfeel. But he was also hungerful: feeding on him, an unwholesome hunger. He had feeded maybe 24 ante-hours, maybe 36. He unknowed, never would know, if it had been AM or PM when they stopped him. Post-stop, he had been unfeeded.

He sitted as unmoving as possible on the unbroad bench, with his hands crossed on his knee. He had learned to sit unmoving. If he moved, they loudspeaked at him from the telescreen. But the hungering for feed was growing in him. What he wanted was a piece of bread. He thinked that there were a few breadcrusts inpocket of his coveralls. It was even possible—he thinked this because time-to-time something touched his leg—there maybe a sizable piece of crust there. In the end, his hunger overcomed his terror; he inpocketed his hand.

'Smith!' loudspeaked the telescreen. '6079 Smith! Hands outpockets!'

He resitted unmoving, his hands crossed on his knee.

Post-stop, they had taked him to another place, maybe a prole prison. He unknowed how long he was there. Without clocks or daylight it was difficult to number the time. It was a loud, doubleplusungood-smelling place, a room nearsame the room he was now in, but doubleplusunclean and everytime crowded by 10 to 15 persons. The majority were prole crimers, but there were a few politcrimers. He sitted, unspeakful, crowded by unclean bodys, overthinkful of the terror and unjoy in his belly, uninterested but watching the shocking unsameways of the politcrimers and other crimers.

The politcrimers were always unspeakful and terrorful, but the crimers cared nothing for anybody. They loudspeaked unclean-words at the safeguards, warred, overpowerful, when their things were taked, writed unclean-words on the floor, taked feed from unwatched-places in their wear, and even counter-loudspeaked the telescreen when it attempted to reorder the crowd. Otherwise, some crimers were unenemyful to the safeguards and called them othernames thru the spy-hole in the door. The safeguards were patienceful with the prole crimers, even when they handled them powerfulwise.

The proles speaked about the joycamps. It was OK in the camps, Smith heared, if you had good contacts and knowed the bylaws. There were kickbacks, freemarketeering of every type, samesexcrimes, sexcrime dealing, unlawful harddrink maked from potatos. The goodest positions were gived to the prole crimers; crime-group members and killers were the highest level. All the unclean low-level work was done by the politcrimers.

There was always a come-and-go of prisoners: drug-pushers, robbers, freemarketeers, harddrinkers, sexcrime dealers. Some of the harddrinkers were so powerful that the other prisoners togethered to overpower them. An oversize woman, about age60, with doubleplusbig breasts and unthin whitehair was carryed in, kicking and loudspeaking, by 4 safeguards, who holded her arms-and-legs. They unweared her boots and dropped her on Smith. The woman upped herself, loudspeaked 'F'ck'n' pi's!' then feeled she was sitting on something, and moved off Smith's knees onto the bench.

'So'ry, luv,' she prolespeaked. 'I 'ou'dn't 'a' sit 'n y', 'nly t' f'ck'rs t'row'd m' 'ere. 'ey dono 'ow to tre' a 'oman, d' t'ey?' She stopped, touched her breasts, and belched. 'So'ry, I ain' m's'lf.'

She leaned over and outstreamed throwup, fullwise, on the floor.

'Tha's go'd'r,' she speaked, leaning on the wall with unopened eyes. 'Ne'er 'nthr'p, tha's wha'. Ge' 't up whi' it's ne' 'n yo'r bel'.'

She relifed, turned to rewatch Smith and speedwise joyfaced him. She placed a plusbig arm round his shoulder and pulled him to her, breathing harddrink and throwup into his face.

'W' 's y'r n'me, luv?'

'Smith'

'Smit'?' Tha' 's 'nus'al. M' n'me's Smit' 'ls'. W'y, I m'yb' y'r p'ren'!'

She maybe, thinked Smith, his parent. She was about the correct age and body-type, and persons semi-changed 20 post-years in joycamp.

Nobody else speaked to him. The prole crimers diswatched the *polits* with a halfhearted unluv. The politcrimers were terrorful of speaking to anybody, of speaking to each other. Only onetime, when 2 Party members, both womans, were sitting pressed together on the bench, he overheared, amid the loudspeakers, a few speedful unloudspeaked words and a reference to 'Room 101,' which he disunderstanded.

Maybe 2 or 3 ante-hours, they had bringed him here to the mirror-white room. The unsharp unjoy in his belly never leaved, but sometimes it growed gooder and sometimes ungooder. When it growed ungooder he thinked only of his bellyfeel and his hunger for feed. When it growed gooder, terror taked hold of him.

He nearwise unthinked of Julia. He was unable to think of her. He luved her and would not betray her; but that was only true, knowed as he knowed true math answers. He unfeeled luv for her, and he nearwise unthinked what was happening to her. He thinked manytimes of O'Brien, with a flashing hope. O'Brien maybe knowed he was in prison. The Brotherhood, he had speaked, never attempted to save its members. But there was the razor; they would send the razor if they were able to. The safeguard would speed into the room, but 5 ante-seconds the razor would have knifed into him with a cold fire, and even the fingers that holded it would be knifed to the bone. But with his unhealthful body, shaking from the unbiggest unjoy, he unknowed if he would use the razor. It was undifficulter to exist second-to-second for another 10 minutes of life, even when he knowed the ending.

Sometimes he attempted to number the mirror-white squares in the room walls. It should be undifficult, but he always disnumbered at sometime. Manytimes he thinked about where he was, and what time of day it was. He feeled it was pluslight outside, then post-second he feeled it was plusunlight. In this place, he knowed, the lights would never off. It was the place without unlight: he knowed now why O'Brien recognized the reference. In Miniluv there were no windows. His room maybe at the heart of the building or on the outer wall; it maybe sublevel10 or level30. He moved in-mind place-to-place, and attempted to bellyfeel if he was high in the air or deep sublevel.

The sound of marching boots outside. The metal door opened with a bang. A youthful officer—a thin black-uniform man in allover new leather, whose white flatface was nearsame a mask—stepped speedwise and orderful thru the doorway. He hand-moved to the safeguards outside to bring in the prisoner. The poemer Ampleforth unspeedwalked into the room. The door rebanged unopen.

Ampleforth moved side-to-side, as tho thinking there was an outdoor, and then started to walk up-down the room. He yet unwatched Smith. His worried eyes were watching the walls overhead Smith. He was unshoed; big, unclean toes outing holes in his socks. He was unrazored, nearsame a strongarm crimer, but his big unpowerful body and unstrong moves were uncrimerful.

Smith unsleeped himself from his halfhearted feelings. He wanted to speak to Ampleforth, tho he would be exposed to the telescreen loudspeaker. It was possible that Ampleforth had the razor.

'Ampleforth'

The telescreen unloudspeaked. Ampleforth stopped, shocked. His eyes unspeedwise finded Smith.

'Smith! You also!'

'What are you in for?'

'Truewise,' He sitted on the bench opposite Smith. 'There's only 1 crime, isn't there?'

'And you've done it?'

'I have.'

He placed a hand to his forehead and pressed, attempting to remember something:

'These things happen. I've been able to remember a—possible—crimethink. It was a misthink. We were producing poems. I OKed an unword. It was unpossible to change the line. For days I had tracked it, mindful. There *wasn't* another word.'

His face changed, nearwise joyful, a teacher who has finded something unuseful. The unableful feeling goed. Thinkful uncold lighted his unclean face.

'Do you know what time of day it is?' Smith questioned.

Ampleforth rewatched, shockful. 'I had near unthinked about it. They stopped me—maybe 2 ante-days—maybe 3.' His eyes speedwise moved round the walls, as tho he half-thinked to find a window somewhere. 'AM-PM, this place is the same. I don't know how we're able to number the hours.'

They speaked half-heartful for a few minutes, then the telescreen loudspeaked at them to be unspeakful. Smith sitted unloud, his hands crossed. Ampleforth, overbig to sit on the unbroad bench, moved side-to-side, his long thin hands round 1 knee, then round the other. The telescreen loudspeaked at him to stay unmoving. Time moved. 20 minutes, 1 hour—it was difficult to number. There was the sound of boots outside. Smith's belly unbigged. Now, later, maybe 5 post-minutes, maybe now, the sound of boots would mean that his time had come.

The door opened. The flatface youthful officer stepped into the room. With an unbig hand-move he arrowed Ampleforth: 'Room 101.' He marched out crosswise between the safeguards, his face worryed, but misunderstanding.

Post-longtime, the unjoy in Smith's belly relifed. His mind goed round-and-round on the same track, nearsame a ball dropping and redropping into the same series of holes. He had only 6 thinks:

unjoy in his belly
piece of bread
questions
O'Brien
Julia
razor

Another bodyful micro-shake in his belly, the heavy boots were coming. The door opened, and powerful cold air streamed into the room, as Parsons walked in. He was wearing light-brown pants and sportshirt. Smith was shocked into self-disremembering.

'*You* here!'

Parsons gived Smith a speedwise eye, uninterested and unshocked, only unjoyful. He started walking crosswise, up-down, unable to stay unmoving. Everytime he straightened his knees, it was clear they were shaking. His eyes were plusopen and watchful, as tho he was unable to unwatch something mid-ground.

'What're you in for?' questioned Smith.

'Crimethink!' speaked Parsons, nearwise unjoyspeaking, both shameful and terrorful that the word was used on him.

He stopped opposite Smith and started heartful speaking to him: 'I haven't done anything—only crimethink, which I'm unable to crimestop. I know they give you a trial. O, they're true to their word! They know my record, don't they? *You* know the type of Party member I was. Not an ungood member, in my way. Not brainful, but goodthinkful. I attempted to do my goodest for the Party. I'll get off with 5 years, don't you think? Or even 10 years? I'll make myself useful in joycamp.'

'Are you shameful?' questioned Smith.

'I'm shameful!' loudspeaked Parsons, underful, speedwise watching the telescreen. 'You don't think the Party would stop an unshameful man, do you?' His frogface now becomed unexcited and overfull. 'Crimethink is a terrorful thing,' he speaked, self-important. 'It's trickful, able to get hold of you unknowing. Do you know how it getted hold of me? In my sleep! Yes, that's true. There I was, working away, attempting to do my workpiece—never knowed I had any ungood stuff in my mind. And then I started sleepspeaking. Do you know what they heared me speaking?'

He downspeaked, as somebody speaking unclean-words.

' "Down with BB!" Yes, I speaked that! Respeaked it over-and-over-and-over. Between you and me, I'm joyful they stopped me. Do you know what I'm going to speak when I go to trial? "Thank you. Thank you for saving me." '

'Who informed on you?'

'It was my unbig girl,' speaked Parsons with an unjoyful pride. 'She heared me thru the door, heared what I was speaking, and goed to Thinkpol post-day. Goodthinkful for a youth of age07! I'm prideful of her. It shows I teached her the correct spirit, anyway.'

'Smith!' loudspeaked the telescreen. '6079 Smith! Uncover your face. All faces uncovered.' Smith uncovered his face.

Parsons was taked away. Prisoners comed-and-goed. A woman was sended to Room 101 and, Smith watched, she unbigged and changed color when she heared the number. A time comed when, if it had been AM when he was bringed here, it was PM; or if it had been PM, then it was AM. There were 6 prisoners in the room, mans and womans. All sitted unmoving. Opposite Smith, a man with a toothful face, nearsame some big animal, and big cheeks, as tho he had feed, unwatched, in his mouth. His white-gray nerveful eyes moved speedwise face-to-face and turned away when he catched somebody's eye.

The door opened, and another prisoner inned, sending speedful cold thru Smith. He was a prole-type coldface man, maybe a machineer, but his face was doubleplusthin, plusshockful. It was nearsame a skull. Because of the thin mouth, his eyes were overbig and full of a killing, ever-warful disluv of somebody or something.

The man sitted on the bench near Smith. Smith unrewatched him, but the unjoyful skullface was clear in his mind, as tho it was straight-front of his eyes. Speedwise he knowed what was uncorrect. The man was becoming unlifeful from overhunger. Everybody in the room samethinked nearsametime. There was a plusunbig moving allway round the bench.

The eyes of the toothful man moved speedwise to the skullface man, then turned away, shameful, then returned, unstoppable. He started to move, unsitful. He standed, unspeedwise moved crosswise thru the room, inpocketed his coveralls and, shameful, outed an unclean piece of bread for the skullface man. A warful overloud oversound from the telescreen. The toothful man jumped in his tracks. The skullface man speedwise pushed his hands behind his back, showing that he untaked the give.

'Bumstead!' loudspeaked the telescreeen. '2713 Bumstead! Drop that piece of bread!'

2713 dropped the piece of bread.

'Stay where you are,' loudspeaked the telescreen. 'Face the door, unmoving.'

2713 followed the orders. His big cheeks were shaking, uncontrolled. The door banged open. The youthful officer inned and sidestepped, and an untall safeguard with oversize arms and shoulders outstepped from behind him. A plusunloud unjoyspeaking, which was unthinkful, outed from 2713. The other prisoners sitted unmoving, their hands crossed on their knees. 2713 reupped to his place on the bench. His eyes speedwise moved face-to-face, plusshameful, as tho attempting to find how the others disluved him for being shamed.

With an unbig hand-move the officer arrowed the skullface man:

'Room 101'

There was an inbreath and exciteful moves at Smith's side. The man had self-throwed to the floor, on his knees with hands together.

'Officer!' he loudspeaked. 'Untake me to that place! Haven't I speaked to you about everything? What else do you want to know? There's nothing I'd unanswer, nothing! Question me, and I'll answer straight off. Write it down and I'll sign it—anything! Not Room 101!'

'Room 101,' respeaked the officer.

The man's skullface, pluswhite, changed to a color Smith thinked unpossible. It was 100% green.

'Not Room 101!' he reloudspeaked. 'Is there somebody else you want me to inform on? Speak the name, and I'll answer anything!'

'Room 101,' doublerespeaked the officer.

The man watched the other prisoners, terrorful, as tho thinking he was able to replace another person in his place. His eyes watched the face of 2713. He arrowed out a thin arm.

'That's who you should to be taking, not me! You unheared what he was speaking. *He's* antiParty, not me.' The safeguards watched as the man doubleplusloudspeaked. 'You unheared him! Something was disrepaired with the telescreen. *Him.* Take him, not me!'

The strong safeguards taked him by the arms. But he holded the metal bench supports and started an unwordful animalful loudspeaking. The safeguards pulled him, but he ever-holded the supports, shockful strong. For maybe 20 seconds, they were pulling at him. The prisoners sitted, unloud, their hands crossed on their knees, watching straight-front of them. The safeguards pulled him up to standing. The man was leaded out, walking unsmoothful, with head down, all the heart goed out of him.

Doublepluslongtime. If it was PM when the skullface man was awayed, it was AM: if AM, it was PM. Smith was single, and had been single for ante-hours. Unjoyful of sitting on the unbroad bench, manytimes he unsitted and walked up-down, unreproved by the telescreen. The bread piece layed where 2713 had dropped it. At the start, it was difficult to unwatch it, but later water- replaced feed-hunger. His mouth was doubleplusmalfeeling. The machine sound and the unchanging whitelight maked him unstrong, an unfull feeling inside his head. He standed, because the unjoy in his bones was over-unjoyful, and then resitted speedwise, because he was lightheaded and unable to stay standing. Whenever his body was undercontrol, the terror returned. Sometimes with an outwhiteful hope he thinked of O'Brien and the razor. It was possible the razor maybe in his feed, if he were ever feeded.

Plusunhopeful, he thinked of Julia. Somewhere she was maybe plusungooder than he. She maybe loudspeaking, disjoyful. He thinked: 'If I was able to save Julia, would I do it? Yes, I would.' But that was only in his mind, thinked because he knowed he should think it. He unfeeled it. In this place, he was unable to feel anything. And was it possible? But that question was yet unanswerable.

The boots were returning. The door opened. O'Brien inned.

Smith upstanded. The shock of watching O'Brien maked him over-uncareful. For time01 in ante-years, he disremembered the telescreen.

'They stopped you also!' he loudspeaked.

'They stopped me ante-longtime,' speaked O'Brien with an unstrong, nearwise sheepful, blackwhite. He sidestepped and a safeguard outstepped from behind him.

'You knowed this, Smith,' speaked O'Brien. 'Don't be untrue to yourself. You did know it—you've always knowed it.'

Yes, he knowed it now, he had always knowed it. A question was answered. There are no heros, no heros, he thinked over-and-over.

chapter02

He was laying on something that feelednearsame a wood bed, except it was higher from the floor and he was strapped down, so he was unable to move. The light was stronger than usual on his face. O'Brien was standing at his side, downwatching him, serious. On the otherside, a man in whitecoat, holding a needle.

Even when his eyes were open, he watched the room only unspeedwise. He feeled as tho he had swimmed up to this room from some otherworld, an underwater world deep under it. How long he was down there, he unknowed. Post-stop, he had unknowed sunlight, and his memory was on-and-off. There had been times when knowing, even knowing that he had sleeped, had stopped and restarted with blanks of days or weeks or only seconds, there was noway of knowing.

He remembered another room with a wood bed, wall-shelf, and metal sink, and meals of plusuncold stew and bread and sometimes coffee. He remembered an enemyful hairstyler coming to razor his chin and knife his hair, and unfeeling workers in whitecoats, watching his heartsounds, touching his body, upturning his eyelids, running ungentle fingers over him, and gunning needles into his arm to make him sleep.

His questioners weren't black-uniform strongarms, but Party goodthinkers: unbig round mans with speedful moves and flashing eyeglasses, who worked on him in series, overtime, for—he thinked, he was unable to know 100%—10 hours or 12 hours. Other questioners watched, so he was ever- and over-shamed, to break his power of arguing and reasoning. Unending questions, on-and-on, hours-and-hours, tricking him, overturning everything he speaked, shaming him at every step, untrue and self-opposite, so he unjoyspeaked from shame and nerves.

Sometimes he would outstream tears manytimes in a single session. They loudspeaked at him, but sometimes they speedwise changed their questions, questioned him in the name of the Party and BB, questioned him unjoyfulwise, if he was trueheartful to the Party and wanted to undo the ungood he had done? When his nerves were breaked, even that question was able to down him to unjoyful tears. In the end the questions breaked him 100%. He becomed a mouth that speaked, a hand that signed, whatever was wanted of him. He only thinked about finding what they wanted him to answer, and then answering it speedwise. He answered questions about his crimes:

crime01 killing, parent
crime02 killing, spouse
crime03 robbing public moneys, to deal on freemarket
crime04 respeaking military info, Recdep
crime05 workstop, every type, thru onwork harddrinking
crime06 betraying the true, Minitrue
crime07 writing untrue reports, Recdep, from year68
crime08 crimethinks, otherworld
crime09 crimethinks, ownlife
crime10 sexcrimes, freemarket
crime11 sexcrimes, underage girl
crime12 contact with Goldstein, thru the book
crime13 member of underground organization, with comrades Julia,
       Syme, Parsons, Ampleforth and other persons

It was undifficult to answer everything and inform on everybody. And it was all true. Crimethinking and crime-acting were the same. He had been an enemy of the Party.

There were also memorys of another type. They outstanded in his mind, disconnected, nearsame pictures with black all-round them:

He was in a room which maybe unlight or light, but he was able to watch only double-eyes. A machine was clicking unspeedwise and timewise. The eyes growed bigger and pluslightful. Speedwise he outstreamed, inned the eyes, and was indrinked.

He was strapped into a chair rounded by telescreens and overlights. A man in whitecoat was reading the screens. The sound of heavy boots outside. The door banged open. The flatface officer marched in, followed by 2 safeguards. 'Room 101.' The man in whitecoat unturned round. He unwatched Smith; he was watching only the screen.

He was rolling down a doubleplusbig hallway, 1km broad, full of plusbeautyful gold light, overjoyspeaking and loudspeaking answers doubleplus. He was answering everything, even unquestioned questions. He was speaking about the history of his whole life to persons who ante-knowed it. With him were safeguards, other questioners, mans in whitecoats, O'Brien, Julia, Charrington, all rolling down the hallway together and loudspeaking with joyspeak. Some terrorful thing, which had been inbedded in the future, was jumped over and unhappened. Everything was OK, everything in his life was exposed, understanded.

He was starting up from the wood bed, half-thinking he heared O'Brien. All thru his questioning, tho he had unwatched him, he had feeled that O'Brien was at his elbow, watchful but unwatched. It was O'Brien who was ordering everything.

It was O'Brien who ordered when Smith should have a break, when he should be feeded, when he should sleep, when the drugs should be streamed into his arm. It was he who questioned and helped the answers. He was the strongarm, he was the safeguard, he was the questioner, he was the unenemy. And sometime—Smith disremembered if it was in drug-sleep, or usual sleep, or unsleep—somebody speaked in his ear:

'Don't worry, Smith; you're in my safeguard. For 7 years I have overwatched you. Now the overturning has come. I'll save you, I'll make you 100% correct.'

He unknowed if it was O'Brien; but it was the same speaker that speaked to him, 'We'll meet in the place where there's no unlight,' in that other dream, 7 ante-years.

He disremembered the end of his questioning. There was a blacktime and—now—the room had unspeedwise shaped itself round him. He was on his back, unable to move. His body was strapped down everywhere. Even the back of his head was holded by something. O'Brien was downwatching him, serious and unjoyful. His face, underwatched, was unsmooth and outweared, with dark undereyes and lines from nose to chin. He was older than Smith had thinked; he was maybe age48 or age50.

'I speaked to you, that if we remeeted it would be here.'

'Yes'

'Don't speak to me untrue, or attempt to avoid the questions in anyway, or be under-thinkful. Do you understand?'

'Yes'

O'Brien's face becomed minusserious. He reweared his eyeglasses, thinkfulwise, and walked, up-down. When he speaked, he was gentle and patienceful, nearsame a teacher speaking with a schooler.

'I'm taking time with you, Smith, because you're useful. You know what's uncorrect with you. You've knowed it ante-years, tho you've warred with that self-knowledge. You're out of your mind. You have a nonworking memory. You're unable to remember true events, and you give reasons for remembering other events which never happened. Goodluck for you, we're able to repair it. You've never self-repaired, because you undoublethinked and unattempted to change your mind. Even now, I know, you're holding onto your dishealthful thinking. Here's an example: Is Oceania now at war?'

'When I was stopped, Oceania was at war.'

'Good. And Oceania has forever been at war, have we not?'

Smith breathed. He opened his mouth to speak, and then unspeaked. He was unable to take his eyes away from the screen.

'Be true, Smith. *Your* true. Speak to me about what you think you remember.'

'I remember that 1 ante-week I was stopped, we weren't at war. We weren't at war. The war had stopped 4 ante-years. 4 ante-years...'

O'Brien stopped him with a hand-move.

Smith was downhearted. That was doublethink. He feeled plusunpowerful. If he 100% knowed that O'Brien was untrue, it would be unimportant. But it was possible that O'Brien truewise disremembered. And if so, then he would have disremembered withholding memory of it, and disremembered the act of disremembering. How was Smith able to know it was a trick? Maybe that displacement in the mind was able to happen: that was the doublethinking that overpowered him.

O'Brien was downwatching him, thinkful, ever-nearsame a teacher working with a headstrong but hopeful schooler.

'There's a Party trueword about the control of the past. Respeak it.'

' "Who controls the past controls the future: who controls the present controls the past," ' respeaked Smith, dutyful.

' "Who controls the present controls the past," ' respeaked O'Brien, updowning his head with an unspeedful OK. 'Is it your thinking, Smith, that the past truewise exists?'

The feeling of doubleplusunpower redowned Smith. He unknowed if 'yes' or 'no' was the answer that would save him; he even unknowed which answer he thinked was true.

O'Brien joyfaced unbigwise. 'You're an undeep thinker, Smith. You've unthinked about what is meaned by *exist*. I'll speak carefulwiser. Does the past exist, as a solid, in a place? Is there somewhere, a place, a world of solid things, where the past is happening?'

'No'

'Then where does the past exist, if it exists?'

'In records. It's writed down.'

'In records. And...?'

'In the mind. In memory.'

'In memory. We, the Party, control all records, and we control all memory. Then we control the past.'

'But how are you able to stop persons from remembering things? It's unvolunteerful. It's ownlife. How are you able to control memory? You've uncontrolled my memory!'

'The opposite,' O'Brien's face was reserious. '*You* have uncontrolled it. That's what has bringed you here. You're here because you're unable to self-shame, to self-control. You wouldn't do the work to become sane. You wanted to stay unsane, a minority of 1. Only the controlled mind is able to be true, Smith. You think the world is something outside, existing in its ownlife. You also think the world is clear-watched, unquestionable. When you trick yourself into thinking that you're watching something, you think that everybody is watching the samething. But I speak to you, Smith, the true world isn't outside the mind. The world exists inside the mind, and *nowhere* else. Not in a single mind, which misthinks and is later unlifeful; only in the Party mind, which groupthinks and is everlifeful. Whatever the Party holds to be true, is true. It's unpossible to watch the world, except by watching thru the eyes of the Party. That's what you must relearn, Smith. You need to self-vaporize and self-control your blackwhite mind. You must be unprideful to become sane.'

He stopped for a few seconds, as tho wanting Smith to think about what he'd been speaking.

'Do you remember writing in your daybook, "2 + 2 = 4?" '

'Yes'

O'Brien upped his lefthand, its back to Smith, with the fingers out.

'How many fingers am I holding up, Smith?'

'4'

'And if the Party speaks: it is not 4, but 5—then how many?'

'4...'

The word ended with a sharp inbreath and sweat comed out allover Smith's body. O'Brien watched him, the fingers out.

'How many fingers, Smith?'

'4'

'How many fingers, Smith?'

'4! 4! What else? 4!'

The heavy serious face and the fingers fulled his eyes. The fingers standed in front of his eyes: oversize, unclear, and shaking.

'How many fingers, Smith?'

'4! Stop it, stop it! How are you able to requestion? 4! 4!'

'How many fingers, Smith?'

'5! 5! 5!'

'No, Smith, that's unuseful. You're being untrue. You think there are 4. How many fingers?'

'4! 5! 4! Anything you want...'

Speedwise he was sitting up with O'Brien's arm round his shoulders. He maybe sleeped for a few seconds. The straps that holded his body were untight. He feeled pluscold, he was shaking uncontrolled, his tooths were clicking, the tears were rolling down his cheeks. He holded onto O'Brien nearsame a baby, joyed by the heavy arm round his shoulders. He felt that O'Brien was his safeguard, and that O'Brien would save him.

'You're an unspeedful learner, Smith,' speaked O'Brien, gentle.

'How am I able to blackwhite it?' he unjoyspeaked. 'How am I able to blackwhite what is in front of my eyes? 2 + 2 = 4.'

'Sometimes, Smith. Sometimes 5. Sometimes 3. Sometimes all those numbers. You must work harder. It's difficult to become sane.'

He placed Smith on the bed. The straps on his arms-and-legs retightened, but the shaking stopped, leaving him only unstrong and cold. O'Brien moved his head at the man in whitecoat, who had standed unmoving during the questioning. The man in whitecoat downfaced and watched Smith's eyes, heared his heartsound, an ear on his chest, touched here-and-there, then he updowned to O'Brien.

'Renumber. How many fingers, Smith?'

He unopened his eyes this time. He knowed the fingers were there: 4. Then he opened his eyes and watched O'Brien.

'4. I think there are 4. I would number 5, if I was able to. I'm attempting to renumber 5.'

'Which do you want: to speak 5, or to truewise watch 5?'

'Truewise to watch them.'

'Renumber. How many fingers am I holding up, Smith?'

Smith was unable to remember, on-and-off, what was happening. Behind his plusunopen eyes, fingers were moving, dancing in-and-out, going behind each other and returning. He was attempting to number them, he disremembered why. He knowed only that it was unpossible to number them, because of the shadow between 5 and 4.

When he opened his eyes, he finded that he was watching the samething. Unnumbered fingers, nearsame moving trees, were streaming everyway, crossing and recrossing. He reunopened his eyes.

'I unknow. I unknow. 4, 5, 6—true, I don't know.'

'Gooder.'

A needle inned Smith's arm. Nearwise in the same millisecond, a joyful healthful uncold overspread his body. The unjoy was half-disremembered. He opened his eyes and upwatched O'Brien, thankful. Watching the heavy lined face, unbeautyful and knowing, his heart overturned. If he had been able to move, he would have touched O'Brien's arm. He had never luved him as deep as now.

The feeling, that it was unimportant if O'Brien was an unenemy or an enemy, had returned. O'Brien was a person he was able to speak with; he understanded Smith. O'Brien had questioned him to the edge of being sane. They were unenemys. Somewhere, tho the words maybe unspeaked, there was a place where they were able to meet and speak. O'Brien was downwatching him, maybe thinking samething in his own mind. He speaked in a smooth conversationful way:

'Do you know where you are, Smith?'

'I unknow. I think in Miniluv.'

'Do you know how long you've been here?'

'I unknow. Days, weeks, months—I think it's months.'

'And why do you think that we bring persons to this place?'

'To make them answer questions.'

'No!' O'Brien outspeaked, doubleplusunsame, and his face speedwise becomed serious and excited.

'No! Not only to get your answers, not only to teach you. Should I speak to you about why we have bringed you here? To repair you! To make you sane! Will you understand, Smith, that nobody we bring to this place leaves our hands unrepaired? We're uninterested in your unthinkful crimes. The Party is uninterested in the outer act; the inner mind is all we care about. We don't only break our enemys, we change them. Do you understand what I mean by that?'

He was over Smith. His face oversize because it was near, and doubleplusunbeautyful because it was underwatched. And it was full of an overjoy, a saneful fire. Smith's heart reunbigged. If it had been possible, he would have downed deeper into the bed. But O'Brien turned away. He walked, up-down. Then he respeaked minuspowerfulwise:

'We undo misthink. All answers speaked here are true. We make them true. Post-life, crimethinkers unbetray the Party. Stop thinking that future generations will clear your name, Smith. Future generations will doubleminus unhear your name. You'll be 100% blanked from the stream of history. We'll change you to vapor and flash you into the stratosphere. Nothing will exist of you, not a name in a record, not a memory in anybody's brain. You'll be vaporized in the past and in the future. You will never have existed.'

Then why question me? thinked Smith, with speedful unjoy. O'Brien stopped mid-step, as tho Smith had speaked to him. His big unbeautyful face comed nearer, with the eyes unbigger.

'You're thinking: we plan to vaporize you, and nothing you speak or do will make any unbig change—so why do we take the time to question you? That's what you're thinking, correct?'

'Yes'

O'Brien joyfaced unbigwise. 'You're a nonworker, Smith, unproducing. You're an unclean thing that must be cleaned up. Final, when you stop warring antiParty, it must be in your own mind. We don't vaporize ungoodthinkers because they crimethink; if they stay crimethinkful, we never vaporize him. We change them, we inprison their inner mind, we reshape them. We fire all doublepusungood and all daydreams; we bring them to our side, not in body only, but truewise: heart and mind. We make them 1 of us. We make their brains 100% correct. Everybody is cleaned all-clean. Nothing stays in them, except unjoy for what they have done, and luv of BB.'

He speaked nearwise dreamful. The overjoy, the sane overjoy, was in his face. He isn't playacting, thinked Smith, he isn't even blackwhiting. He knows every word he speaks is true. What downed Smith was knowing his mind was unbigger. He watched O'Brien's heavy body walking here-and-there. He was a person ever-bigger than him. Smith was unable to think of anything that O'Brien hadn't ante-thinked, -watched, and -unOKed. His mind holded Smith's mind *within* his. So was it true that O'Brien was unsane? It must be he, Smith, who was unsane.

'Unthink that you'll self-save, Smith. What happens to you here is forever. Understand that. We'll break you; there's unreturning. Things will happen to you here, from which you're unable to recover. You'll be unfull. We'll unfull you, and then we'll full you with ourself.'

O'Brien stopped and downwatched him. He hand-signed to the man in whitecoat. A heavy machine was pushed into place behind Smith's head. O'Brien sitted beside the bed, so his face was nearsame level with Smith's.

'3000,' he overspeaked Smith's head, to the man in whitecoat.

Something soft and wet self-clipped to the sides of Smith's head. He shaked with terror. A new thing was coming. O'Brien placed a hand on his, nearwise unenemyful.

'Watch my eyes.'

An overpowering blast, unheared, unsoundful—a white flash of light. Smith wasn't dishealthful, only downed. Tho he had been laying on his back when it happened, he had the unusual feeling that he'd been knocked into that position. A doubleplus, not unjoyful, hit had hammered him flat. And something happened inside his head. As his eyes recovered, he remembered who he was, and where he was, and recognized the face that was watching his; but somewhere there was a big unfull place, as tho a piece had been taked out of his brain.

'It won't stay this way,' speaked O'Brien. 'Watch my eyes. Is Oceania at war?'

Smith thinked. He knowed what was meaned by *Oceania* and that he was a person in Oceania. He also remembered the enemy, but who was at war with who? He unknowed. He unknowed there was any war.

'I disremember.'

'Oceania is at war. Do you remember that now?'

'Yes'

'Oceania has forever been at war. Ante-start of your life, ante-Party, ante-history, nonstop forever war, always the same war. Do you remember that?'

'Yes'

'A few ante-minutes, I upped the fingers of my hand. You watched 5 fingers. Do you remember that?'

'Yes'

O'Brien upped the fingers of his lefthand.

'There are 5 fingers there. Do you watch 5 fingers?'

'Yes'

And he did watch them, for a millisecond. He watched 5 fingers, and they weren't misshaped. Then everything returned to usual, and terror, unluv, and crimethink returned. But there had been a time—he unknowed how long, 30 seconds maybe—of lightful goodthinking, when every new answer from O'Brien had fulled a blank place and becomed 100% true, and when 2 + 2 = 3, undifficult, or 2 + 2 = 5, if that answer was needed. It was now outwhited; he was unable to rethink it, but he was able to remember it, as he remembered sometime in his ante-lifetime, when he was an unsame person.

'You know now that it's possible.'

'Yes'

O'Brien standed, satisfyed. On his left, Smith watched the man in whitecoat prep a needle. O'Brien turned to Smith with a joyface. He reweared his eyeglasses.

'Do you remember writing in your daybook that it was unimportant if I was an unenemy or an enemy, because I was a person who understanded you, and you're able to be speak to me? You were correct. I enjoy speaking to you. Your mind speaks to me, nearsame my own mind, except that you happen to be unsane. As we end this session, do you want to question *me*?'

'What have you done with Julia?'

'She betrayed you, Smith.' O'Brien rejoyfaced. 'Speedwise—100%. I have only sometimes watched a person join us so speedwise. You would nearwise unrecognize her. All her antiParty crimethink, her untrue acts, her ungoodthinking, her unclean think—everything has been fired from her. It was a 100% changeover. Another question.'

'Does BB exist?'

'He exists. The Party exists. BB inbodys the Party.'

'Does he exist in the sameway I exist?'

'You unexist.'

He refeeled unpowerful. He knowed, or was able to think of, the arguments which evidenced his nonexistence; they were goodthink. But was it useful to speak about it? His mind unbigged as he thinked about the unanswerable arguments which O'Brien would use to blank him.

'I think I exist. I know about my ownlife. I was born and I'll unlife. I have arms-and-legs. I full this place. No other solid thing's able to full this sameplace sametime. In that way, does BB exist?'

'It's unimportant. He exists.'

'Will BB ever be unlifeful?'

'No. How would he become unlifeful? Another question.'

'Does the Brotherhood exist?'

'That, Smith, you'll never know. Even if you stay lifeful to age90, you'll unlearn the answer to that question: Yes or No. For your whole lifetime it'll be an unanswered question in your mind.'

Smith layed unspeakful. His chest up-downed unbigwise speedfuller. He had unspeaked question01 that comed into his mind. He must question it, but it was as tho his tongue would unspeak it. There was joy in O'Brien's face. Even his eyeglasses flashed blackwhite. He knows, thinked Smith speedwise, he knows the question! The words bursted out of him:

'What's in Room 101?'

O'Brien's face unchanged. He answered, unfeeling:

'You know what's in Room 101, Smith. Everybody knows what's in Room 101.'

He upped a finger to the man in whitecoat. The session was ended. A needle streamed into Smith's arm. He downed speedwise into deep sleep.

chapter03

'There are 3 levels in your return to the Party.' O'Brien numbered: 'Learning, understanding, and recognizing the true and correct. It's time for you to go to level02.'

As always, Smith was laying on his back. But his straps were untight. They holded him to the bed, but he was able to move his knees, turn his head side-to-side, and up his arms from the elbow. The questions, also, had growed minusterrorful. He was able to avoid straight answers, if he thinked speedwise. When he was ungoodthinkful, O'Brien becomed unjoyful. He disremembered how many sessions there had been. The whole process was a long unknowed time—weeks, maybe—and the times between sessions maybe sometimes days, sometimes only hours.

'As you lay there, you have manytimes thinked—you have even questioned me—why Miniluv gives you longtime sessions and cares about you. And when you were in your own room, you self-questioned. You were able to understand the systems of society, but not the underlaying reasons. Do you remember writing in your daybook: "I understand *how*: I disunderstand *why*"? It was when you thinked about *why* that you questioned if you were sane. You understand *how* the Party stays in power. Now speak to me about *why* we hold onto power. What is our reason? Why should we want power?'

'Go on. Speak,' he plussed, as Smith stayed unspeakful.

But Smith unspeaked for another second, overfeeling unstrong and sleepful. The unbig saneful flash of overjoy returned to O'Brien's face. Smith thinked he knowed what O'Brien would speak: the Party unwanted power for itself, but only for the good of the majority, for the joy of the majority. The Party was the ever-safeguard of the unstrong.

The terrorful thing, for Smith, the terrorful thing was that when O'Brien speaked this, he would also know it and understand it. O'Brien knowed everything. 1,000 times gooder than Smith, he knowed the true world. He understanded all, weighed all. What am I able to do, thinked Smith, to a sane man, who is knowfuller than me, who hears my arguments, and then stays unchanged?

'You're leading us for our own good,' Smith speaked, unstrong. 'You think that persons are unable to lead themselfs, and so...'

'That was unthinkful, Smith, ungoodthinkful!' O'Brien loudspeaked. 'You should know to unspeak that way. Now, I'll speak to you about the answer to my question.'

Smith rewatched O'Brien's unenergyful face. It was big and strong and coldhearted and knowful. He controlled his feelings, and that maked Smith feel unpowerful; but O'Brien's face was unenergyful: dark undereyes, the skin pulled down from the cheekbones. O'Brien leaned over him, unspeedwise bringing his outweared face nearer.

'You're thinking that my face is unyouthful and unenergyful. You're thinking that I speak of power, but I'm unable to stop the breakdown of my own body. Do you disunderstand, Smith, that 1 person is only a single part? A breaked unstrong part means a strong whole animal. Do you self-kill when you knife your hair?'

He turned away from the bed and started rewalking up-down, hand inpocket.

'Thing01 you must understand is only groupthink is true power. A person only has power when they stop being a single person. You know the Party trueword: "Joyful in Work." Have you ever thinked that it's back-to-front? "Work in Joy." Ownlife—unworking—the person is always unjoyful. It must be so, because everybody must unlife, which is the doubleplusbiggest unwin. But if you're able to make your lifetime 100% worktime, if you're able to disownlife, if you're able to be in the Party, so that you *are* the Party, then you're all-powerful and everlifeful.'

'Thing02 for you to understand is that power is power over persons. Over the body and over the mind. Power over things—the world, as you call it—is unimportant. Our control over the world of things is 100%.'

Smith attempted to up to a sitting position, but was only able to move his body unjoyfulwise.

'But how're you able to control things?' Smith outbursted. 'You don't even control the weather or the law of gravity. And there is dishealth and unlife...'

O'Brien unspeaked him with a hand-move. 'We control things because we control the mind. The world is inside the skull. You'll learn by levels, Smith. There's nothing we're unable to do. Shape-changing, flying—anything. I'm able to fly nearsame a bird if I want to. I unwant to, because the Party unwants it. You must cleanup those oldthinks about laws. We make the laws.'

'But you don't! You haven't even overpowered this world. What about the enemy? You've unstopped them yet.'

'Unimportant. We'll stop them when we want to. And if we unstop, what change would it make? We're able to unexistence them. Oceania is the world.'

'But the world itself is only dust. And persons are doubleplusunbig—unpowerful! How long have we been in existence? For 1,000,000s of ante-years the world was unlifeful.'

'Ungoodthink. The world is as old as we are, not older. How is it possible to be older? Nothing exists except thru knowing.'

'But the ground is full of doubleplusoldtime animal bones, which were lifeful here longtime ante-humans.'

'Have you ever watched those bones, Smith? No. Oldthinkers invented them. Ante-humans, there was nothing. Post-humans, if we're even able to end, there will be nothing. Outside humans there's nothing.'

'But everything's outside us. Watch the stars! Some of them are 1,000,000 light-years away. That's forever.'

'What are stars?' speaked O'Brien, uncaring. 'They're pieces of fire a few km away. We're able to go to them if we want to. Or we're able to blank them. The world is mid-everything. The sun and stars go round it.'

Smith reshaked, uncontrollable. This time he unspeaked anything. O'Brien ever-speaked, as tho answering a question:

'Sometimes, that's untrue. When we travel cross the ocean, or when we forecast about the moon, we manytimes find it useful to think the world goes round the sun and the stars are 10,000,000km away. But what of it? Do you think we're unable to produce a double system? The stars are both near or unnear, as we need them. Do you think our mathers are unable to do that? Have you disremembered doublethink?'

Smith unbigged down into the bed. Whatever he speaked, the speedful answer hammered him as a club. But he knowed, he *knowed*, that he was correct. Thinking that nothing exists outside your own mind—there must be someway of showing that it was 100% untrue? Hadn't it been exposed ante-longtime as untrue? There was even a name for it, which he disremembered. O'Brien downwatched him with an unbig joyface.

'I ante-speaked to you, Smith, that you're an undeep thinker. The true power, the power we're warring for AM-PM, isn't power over things, but over persons. There won't be trueheart, except trueheart to the Party. There won't be luv, except the luv of BB. If you want a picture of the future, think of the face of BB—forever.'

He stopped as tho he thinked Smith wanted to speak. Smith attempted to reunbig into the bed. He was unable to speak about anything. His heart was nearsame ice. O'Brien respeaked:

'And remember: it's forever. The face of BB will always be there. This playact, that I have played with you for 7 years, will be replayed over-and-over-and-over, for generations-and-generations, always in sharper ways. Always we'll have the ungoodthinker here, shameful, saved. That's the world we're prepping for, Smith. A world of win-and-win, and win-and-win-and-win: an ever-pressing, pressing, pressing on the nerve of power. You're starting to understand what that world will be. But in the end, you'll understandest it. You'll be OK with it, enjoy it, become it.'

Smith had recovered enough to speak, unstrong: 'You're unable to!'

'What do you mean by those words, Smith?'

'You're unable to produce that type of world. It's a dream. It's unpossible.'

'Why?'

'It's unpossible to lead a civilization with terror and unluv and coldheart. It would never grow.'

'Why not?'

'It would be unlifeful. It would breakdown. It would self-kill.'

'Ungoodthink. You think that unluv is minus than luv. Why? And if it were true, what changes? If we breakdown speedfuller, if we speedup lifetimes until persons are unlifeful at age30, what changes? Do you disunderstand that unlife of the person isn't unlife? The Party is everlifeful.'

As usual, the loudspeaking had hammered Smith to be unpowerful. And he was in terror. But he was unable to stay unspeakful. Unstrong, arguments unexisting, with nothing to uphold him except his unspeakable terror of what O'Brien had speaked, he returned to the mind-war.

'I don't know—I don't care. You'll unwin. Something will overpower you. Life will overpower you.'

'We control life, Smith, at all levels. You're daydreaming there's something called *human*, who will over-feel unjoy and turn antiParty. But we produce humans. We hammer, press, reshape. Persons are all-changeable. Or maybe you've returned to thinking the proles or the workers will standup and overthrow us. Disremember that thinking. They are unpowerful, nearsame animals. Only persons are inside the Party. The others are outside—unimportant.'

'I uncare. In the end they'll overpower you. Unlater-or-later they'll understand what you are, and then they'll rip you to pieces.'

'Any evidence that's happening? Or any reason why it should?'

'No. I think it. I *know* that you'll unwin. There's something—I don't know, some spirit, something—that you'll never overcome.'

'What is this thing that will overpower us?'

'I unknow. The human spirit.'

'And do you think you're human?'

'Yes'

'If you're a human, Smith, you're the final human. Your type is the past; we're the post-generation. Do you understand that you're *single*? You're outside history, you're nonexisting.' His face changed, ungentle. 'And you think yourself over us, with your untrue thinking and unclean crimes?'

'Yes, I think I'm goodest.'

O'Brien was unspeakful. 2 other persons were speaking. Smith recognized 1 of them as himself. It was a soundtrack of the conversation he had with O'Brien, when he joined the Brotherhood. He heared himself pledging:

to speak ever-untrue
to rob
to kill
to self-print money
to push drugs
to deal sexcrimes
to outspread dishealthful sex
to throw acid in a baby's face

O'Brien maked an unbig unpatienceful hand-move, showing this was unuseful. He pushed a button: the loudspeakers stopped and the straps auto-untightened. Smith downed to the floor, unstrong.

'Standup. You're the final human. You're the safeguard of the human spirit. You'll show yourself, to yourself. Unwear your coveralls.'

Smith unclipped the waist-strap that holded his coveralls together. The zipper had been pulled out of them. He disremembered if anytime post-stop he had unweared his coveralls and underwear. Under the coveralls his body was rounded with plusunclean yellow underwear. As he dropped the coveralls to the ground, he watched the 3-side mirror at room-end. He goed to it, then stopped. An unvolunteerful loudspeak outbreaked from him.

'Go on,' speaked O'Brien. 'Stand between the wings of the mirror. Watch how your body moves.'

He had stopped because he was terrorful. An unstraight, gray skeleton thing was coming to him. It was truewise terrorful, and not only because he knowed it was himself. He moved nearer to the mirror. The face outstanded, because of the unstraight body. An unjoyful birdface with an unsmooth forehead running into an unhaired head, an unstraight nose, and hammered cheekbones. His eyes were overpowerful and watchful. The cheeks were lined, the mouth inpulled. It was his ownface, but it was changed, tho he stayed unchanged inside. The feelings it recorded would be unsame what he feeled.

For a second, he thinked that he had grayhair, but it was his head that was gray. Except for his hands and face, his body was gray allover with deep unclean. Here-and-there under the unclean there were red scars and his dishealthful leg had skin coming off it. But the truewise terrorful thing was his over-thin body. His chest was same as a skeleton. The legs had thinned, so the knees were bigger than the thighs. The unstraight backbone was shocking.

The thin shoulders were rounded so as to infall the chest, the boneful neck unstraight from the overweighful skull. He would have thinked it was the body of a man age60, unjoyful and unhealthful.

'You have thinked sometimes,' speaked O'Brien, 'that my face—the face of an Inner Party member—is old and outweared. What do you think of your ownface?'

He taked Smith's shoulder and turned him round so he was facing him.

'Watch the mirror! Plusunclean allover your body. Unclean between your toes. Disgusting open scar on your leg. Do you know that you smell nearsame an animal? You're doubleplusthin. Watch: I'm able to unopen my hand round your forearm, or break your neck nearsame an unbig branch. Do you know that you have dropped 25kg? Even your hair is coming out in handfuls!'

He pulled out some hair from Smith's head. 'Open your mouth. 9, 10, 11 tooths. How many when you comed to us? And the few that stay are dropping out of your head!' He holded 1 of Smith's front tooths in his fingers. Unjoy fulled Smith's jaw. O'Brien pulled out a tooth and throwed it away.

'You're wasting away. You're falling to pieces. What are you? A waste-pile. Now turn round and face the mirror. Are you watching that thing facing you? That's the final human. If you're a human, that's all humans. Now rewear your coveralls.'

Smith started to rewear his coveralls with unspeedful tight moves. Ante-now, he unknowed how thin and unstrong he was. Only 1 think moved in his mind: he had been in this place longer than he thinked. Then speedwise, as he reweared the doubleplusungood wears, a feeling of shameful unjoy for his downed and disrepaired body overcomed him. He downed beside the bed and bursted into tears. He knowed his unbeauty, a pack of bones in plusunclean underwear sitting unjoyspeaking in the doublepluswhitelight. But he was unable to self-stop. O'Brien placed a hand on his shoulder, nearwise unenemyful.

'It won't be forever. You're out of it, whenever you want. You control everything.'

'You did it! You downed me to this!'

'No, Smith, you self-downed to this. You were OK with this, when you turned antiParty. It was all within that act01. Nothing has happened that you unforecasted.'

He stopped, and then respeaked: 'We win, Smith. We have breaked you. You have watched your body in the mirror. Your mind is the same. I unthink you can stay prideful. You have betrayed everybody and everything.'

Smith stopped unjoyspeaking, tho tears were outstreaming his eyes. He upwatched O'Brien. 'I've unbetrayed Julia.'

O'Brien downwatched him thinkfulwise. 'No. No, that's 100% true. You have unbetrayed Julia.'

The usual worship for O'Brien, which was unbreakable, refulled Smith's heart. How knowing, he thinked, how knowing! O'Brien always understanded what was speaked to him. Anybody else in the world would have answered speedwise that he *had* betrayed Julia. He had speaked of everything he knowed about her, her habits, her good-name, her past life; he had answered everything about their meets, all that he had speaked to her and she to him, their freemarket meals, their sexcrimes, their unclear antiParty plans—everything. But, in the way he used the word, he had unbetrayed her. His feelings for her had stayed the same. He had unstopped luving her. O'Brien knowed what he meaned.

chapter04

He was plusgooder. He was growing unthinner and stronger everyday, if it was correct to speak of *days*.

The whitelight and machine sound were ever-same, but this room was gooder than the ante-places. There was a pillow and mattress on the board bed, and an unbig chair. They gave him a bath, and a metal sink, and uncold water for self-cleaning. They gave him new underwear and clean coveralls. They used rehealthful drugs on his dishealthful leg. They pulled his old tooths and gived him new tooths.

Post-weeks or -months, it would be possible now to number the time, if he had any interest in doing so, because he was being feeded at, maybe, orderful times. He was getting, he thinked, 3 meals in 24 hours; sometimes he questioned if he was getting them AM or PM. The feed was good, with meat at every meal03.

They gave him a white notebook and pencil, but he unused it. Even when he was unsleeping he was doubleplusunenergyful. Manytimes he would lay meal-to-meal, nearwise unmoving, sometimes sleeping, sometimes unsleeping into unclear daydreams in which it was overdifficult to open his eyes. He was now habitful of sleeping with a strong light on his face. It unchanged his sleep, except that his dreams were clearer. He dreamed doubleplus all thru this time, and they were always joyful dreams. He was in Gold Country, or he was sitting in oversize plusbeautyful sunlightful houses, with his parent, with Julia, with O'Brien—undoing anything, only sitting in the sun, speaking of joyful things. When he was unsleeping, he thinked about his dreams, unmindful. He unwanted conversation or sidetracks. Only to be ownlife, to be unquestioned, to have enough feed, and to be clean allover, was doubleplussatisfying.

Unspeedwise, he slept unlonger, but he unwanted to off the bed. All he wanted was to lay unloud and feel the strong returning to his body. He would self-touch here-and-there, attempting to know 100% that he was undaydreaming, that his muscles were growing rounder and his skin tighter. Final, he knowed, over-unquestionful, that he was growing unthinner; his thighs were now bigger than his knees.

Unenergyfulwise, he started timeful physed. Unlongtime, he was able to walk 3km, round the room, and his unstraight shoulders growed straighter. He attempted difficulter physeds, and was shocked and shamed to find what things he was unable to do. He was unable to move out of a walk, he was unable to hold his chair out at arm-long, he was unable to stand on 1 leg and undrop to the floor. He sitted down, and with bodyful unjoy in his legs, he was able to up to a standing position. He layed on his belly and attempted to do a pushup. It was unhopeful, he was unable to up 1cm. But in a few days—a few mealtimes—he did it. A time comed when he was able to do it 6 times in series. He started to grow prideful of his body, and to enjoy on-and-off thinking that his face also was regrowing to usual. Only when he placed his hand on his unhaired head did he remember the lined, breaked face that had counter-watched him from the mirror.

His mind growed thinkfuller. He sitted on the wood bed, his back to the wall and the notebook on his knees, and started the thinkful work of relearning.

He had stopped warring. He had been prepped to stop warring for longtime. When he was inside Miniluv—and yes, even when he and Julia had standed unpowerful while the metal loudspeaker from the telescreen speaked to them—he understanded that his attempt to be antiParty was unserious and undeep.

He knowed now that for 7 years Thinkpol had watched him nearsame a bug under glass. There was no act, no word, that they had unwatched; no series of thinks that they had been unable to understand. Even the white dust on the cover of his daybook they had carefulwise replaced. They had played soundtracks to him, showed him photos. Photos of Julia and him. Yes, even photos of their sexcrimes. He was unable to war antiParty. And the Party was correct. It must be true; how was it possible for everlifeful groupthink to misthink? By what evidence was he able to show the Party was uncorrect? Sane was statsful. It was only a question of learning to doublethink as they doublethinked. Only...!

The pencil feeled unthin and unusual in his fingers. He started to write the thinks that comed into his head. He writed in big crosswise words:

JOYFUL IN WORK

Then nearwise unstopping he writed under it:

$$2 + 2 = 5$$

But then there comed a stop. His mind, as tho moving away from something, was unable to deep-think. He knowed that he knowed, but he disremembered it. When he remembered it, it was only by mindful reasoning: it wasn't yet auto-doublethink. He writed:

STRONG IN PARTY

Everything was OK. The past was rectifyable. The past never had been rectifyed. Oceania was at war. Oceania had forever been at war. He remembered remembering opposite things, but those were untrue memorys, products of self-untrue. How undifficult it all was! Only stop warring, and everything else followed. It was nearsame swimming upstream, being pushed back but ever-warring, and then speedwise turning round and going downstream. Nothing had changed except his own mind. The thing happened anyway. He unknowed why he had ever crimethinked. Everything was undifficult, except...!

Anything maybe true. The law of gravity was rectifyable. 'If I wanted,' O'Brien had speaked, 'I'm able to fly nearsame a bird.' Smith worked it out. 'If he *thinks* he flys, and if I sametimewise *think* I watch him flying, then the thing happens.' What knowledge have we of anything, except thru our minds? All happenings are in the mind. Whatever happens in all minds, truewise happens.

It was undifficult to unthink the untrue, and he was safe from undering to it. But he knowed that he should have unthinked it. The mind should have a blank place whenever crimethink showed itself. The crimestop process should be auto-safeguardful.

He started working to self-teach crimestop. He self-questioned—'the Party speaks: the world is flat'—and self-prepped in unknowing or misunderstanding the counter-arguments. It was difficult. He needed doubleplusbig powers of reasoning and doublethinking. The math problem $2 + 2 = 5$ was overcomplex. He needed also a strong speedful mind, able to make the carefullest use of doublethink, and then be unthinkful. Goodthink was as needed as doublethink, and as difficult to learn.

'You control everything,' O'Brien had speaked; but he knowed there was noway to bring relearning nearer. It maybe 10 post-minutes or 10 post-years. He maybe stay for years in this single room, they maybe send him to joycamp, they maybe out him for sometime, as they sometimes did. It was possible the whole playact of his stop and questioning would be reacted allover.

AM—but *AM* was the uncorrect word; maybe it was PM—*Onetime* he was in an unusual joyful daydream. He was walking down the hallway and everything was answered, smoothed out, retogethered. There were no questions, no arguments, no unjoy, no terror. His body was healthful and strong. He walked smoothwise, with a joy of moving and with a feeling of walking in sunlight. He wasn't in the unbroad white Miniluv hallways; he was in the oversize sunlightful hallway, 1km broad, which he had walked in the drug-dream. He was in Gold

Country, following the foot-track thru the field. He feeled the unlong soft grass underfoot and gentle sunlight on his face. At the field-edge were the trees, unbigwise moving, and somewhere the stream with fish in greenwater under the trees.

Speedwise he upped with shockful terror, sweat on his back. He had heared himself sleepspeak:

'Julia! Julia! Julia, my luv! Julia!'

He had daydreamed overfeelful of her. She wasn't only with him, but inside him, as tho she was within his skin. In that second he luved her doubleplus, as when they were together. He knowed that somewhere she was lifeful and needed his help.

He relay on the bed and attempted to self-organize. What had he done?

That outburst wouldn't go unanswered. They would know now, if they had no ante-knowledge, that he was breaking the pledge. He followed the Party, but he unluved the Party. In his daybook-writing days, he had an ungoodthinkful mind behind a goodthinkful mask. Now he had backstepped. In his mind he had stopped warring, but he hoped his inner heart was untouched. He knowed he was untrue, but he wanted to be untrue. They would understand that—O'Brien would understand it. It was all answered in that single sexcrimeful loudspeak. Now he must restart from Ø. It maybe post-years.

He touched his face, attempting to know its new shape: deep lines in his cheeks, cheekbones sharp, nose flat. And, post-self-mirroring, he had been gived new tooths. It was difficult to stay flatface when he unknowed his ownface. Control of the face wasn't enough. He knowed that if he wanted something unwatched, he also must unwatch it. He must know it's there, but it must stay out of mind, unshaped, ever-unnamed. From now, he must doublethink correct; he must feel correct, dream correct.

He unopened his eyes. Self-control was difficulter than mind-control. It was a question of self-downing, self-defacing. He must drop into the uncleanest of unclean. What was the terrorfullest dishealthfullest thing? He thinked of BB. The oversize face, with its heavy black mustache and eyes that followed him, auto-streamed into his mind. What were his true feelings for BB?

The sound of heavy boots in the hallway. The metal door banged open. O'Brien walked into the room. Behind him, the flatface officer and the black-uniform safeguards.

'Up. Come here.'

Smith standed opposite him. O'Brien holded Smith's shoulders between his strong hands and watched him.

'You thinked of being untrue to me. That was unthinkful. Standup straighter. Watch my face.'

He stopped and respeaked in a gentler way:

'You're gooder. There is plusunbig unsane in your mind. It's only heartwise that you're ungooder. Speak to me, Smith—and remember, no untrues; you know I'm always able to find the untrue—speak to me, what are your true feelings for BB?'

'I unluv him.'

'You unluv him. Good. Then the time has come for you to take the final step. You must luv BB. It's unenough to follow him; you must luv him.'

He unholded Smith with an unbig push to the safeguards.

'Room 101'

chapter05

At each level of his questioning he had knowed, or thinked he knowed, where he was in the unwindowful building. Maybe there were unbig changes in the air. The room where he had been questioned by O'Brien was high up near the roof. This place was doubleplussublevel, as deep down as it was possible to go.

It was bigger than the rooms he had been in. But he unfullwise watched round. He was strapped in a chair, so tight that he was able to move nothing, not even his head. Something holded his head from behind, overpowering him to watch straight-front. He was single for a few minutes, then the door opened and O'Brien inned.

'You questioned me onetime, what was in Room 101? I speaked to you: you knowed the answer. Everybody knows it. The thing that's in Room 101 is the ungoodest thing in the world. The ungoodest thing in the world is unsame, person-to-person. Sometimes it's a plusunimportant thing.'

'You're unable to know that!' Smith loudspeaked, with a high and breaked sound. 'You're unable to, you're unable to! It's unpossible.'

'Do you remember that terror from your dreams? There was a blackwall in front of you and an oversound in your ears. There was something terrorful on the otherside of the wall. You knowed that you knowed what it was, but you didn't have the strongheart to pull it into the open.'

'O'Brien!' Smith attempted to control his speaking. 'You know this is unneeded. What is it that you want me to do?'

O'Brien unanswered straight. He speaked in his teacherful way. He watched the room, thinkfulwise, as tho speaking to persons somewhere behind Smith.

'For everybody there's something overstrong—something unthinkable— and you'll do what is ordered of you.'

'But what is it? How am I able to do it, if I don't know what it is?'

Smith was able to hear bloodsong in his ears. He feeled he was sitting in a place, full of sunlight—100% single—a doubleplusbig, flat, unfull field. All sounds comed to him out of the doubleplusunnear. He heared a deep unhopeful unjoyspeak from somewhere outside himself, a series of sharp loudspeaks from overhead. But he over-warred his terror.

To think, to think, even for a millisecond—to think was the only hope. There was a powerful shaking inside his belly, and everything goed black. For a millisecond he was a loudspeaking animal. Yet he comed out of the black holding a think. There was oneway, and only oneway, to self-save. He must displace another person, the *body* of another person.

And then—no, it was only hope, a doubleplusunbig hope. But he had speedwise understanded that in the whole world there was *1 person* who was able to replace him—*1 body*—and he was loudspeaking, terrorful, over-and-over:

'Do it to Julia! Do it to Julia! Not me! Julia! I don't care what you do to her. Not me! Julia! Not me!'

He was dropping down, over-deep, away from Room 101. He was strapped in the chair, but he had dropped thru the floor, thru the walls of the building, thru the world, thru the oceans, thru the atmosphere, to the outer stars—always away, away, away. He was light years away, but O'Brien stayed standing at his side.

chapter06

The Chestnut Tree was near unfull. Sunlight angling thru a window onto dustful tabletops. It was the singleful hour of 15:00. Music outstreamed the telescreens.

Smith sitted in his usual corner, watching an unfull glass. Sometimes he speedwise watched the plusbig face which eyed him from the opposite wall.

BB IS WATCHING YOU

Unordered, a server comed and fulled his glass with Winful Harddrink, shaking in a few drops from a bottle of sugar and cloves, the house-drink of the cafe.

Smith was watching the telescreen. Now only music was outstreaming, but any second there maybe an unusual Minipax newscast. The news from the frontline was terrorful. On-and-off he had been worrying about it all day. The enemy (Oceania was at war. Oceania had forever been at war.) was moving south with terrorful speed. It was time01 in the whole war that Oceania itself was threatened.

A powerful feeling, not terror but an unclear excitement, fired up, then outwhited. He stopped thinking about the war. These days he was unable to think about any subject for over a few seconds. He upped his glass and drinked. As always, the harddrink maked him shake and belch unbigful. The stuff was doubleplusungood. The sugar and cloves, disgusting and unhealthful, were unable to mask the oil smell; and what was ungoodest was the harddrink smell, within him AM-PM, was mixed with the smell of those...

He never named them, even in his mind, and attempted to ever-unwatch them. They were something that he half-knowed, near his face, a smell in his nose. As the harddrink upped in him, he belched thru red-blue lips.

He had growed unthinner post-Miniluv and had recolored—plusrecolored. His face had unthinned, the skin on nose and cheekbones was unsmooth, red, even the unhaired head was overdeep light-red. A server bringed the gameboard and *The Times*, with the page downturned at the game problem. Then, watching Smith's unfull glass, he bringed the harddrink bottle and fulled it. Orders were unneeded; they knowed his habits. The gameboard was always waiting for him, his corner table was always there; even when the place was full, he was single, because nobody wanted to sit near him.

He never numbered his drinks. Sometimes they showed him an unclean piece of paper, which numbered his drinks, but he thinked they under-dealed him. It would be unchanged, if it had been otherwise. He had plenty of money now. He even had work, moneyer than his ante-work.

The music from the telescreen stopped and a loudspeaker started. Smith upped his head to hear. No update from the front. It was only a Miniplenty newscast: in the ante-quarter, the 3YP10 production of boots had been overfulled by 98%.

He readed the game problem and placed the pieces. It was a trickful endgame. 'White to play and win in 2 moves.' Smith upwatched the BB picture. White always wins, he thinked with an unclear otherworldful mind. Always, unexceptful, it's so planned. In no game problem, post-start of the world, has black ever winned. Was it a sign of the unchanging ever-win of Good over Ungood? The doubleplusbig face watched him, full of unexciteful power. White always wins.

The telescreen stopped and spoke in an unsame and seriouser sound: 'Standby for an important update at 15:30. 15:30! This is importantest news. Standby. 15:30!'

The clear-sound music restarted. Smith's heart moved. That was the newscast from the frontline; his animalthink speaked to him: it was ungoodnews coming. All day, unbig exciteful, a doubleplusbig unwin had been in-and-out of his mind. He watched the enemy crowding thru the never-breaked frontline and downstreaming, nearsame bugs. Why had it been unpossible to outthink them?

He upped a white gamepiece and moved it on the board. *There* was the correct move. Even as he watched the black crowd speeding south, he watched another power, togethered but unwatched, speed behind them, knifing them on land and ocean. He feeled that by wanting it he was bringing that other power into existence. But he needed to act speedwise. It would knife Oceania in half. It may mean anything: unwin, breakdown, reorder the world, vaporize the Party!

He inbreathed deep. An unusual mix of feelings—but it wasn't a mix; it was a series of layers; he was unable to know which layer was underest—warred inside him.

The bodyful micro-shake stopped. He replaced the white gamepiece, but he was unable to be serious and read about the game problem. His thinks retravelled, unstraight. Near unthinkful, he writed with his finger in the table dust:

2 + 2 = 5

'They're unable to get inside you,' Julia had speaked. But they were able to get inside him.

'What happens to you here is *forever*,' O'Brien had speaked. That was trueword. There were things, his own acts, from which he was unable to recover. Something was killed in his chest: fired out, cleaned out.

He had meeted Julia post-Miniluv; he had even speaked to her. He knowed they were now uninterested in his doings. He was unwatched. He was able to remeet her, if either of them wanted to. It was by luck that they had meeted. It was in the park, on a doubleplusungood, doublepluscold day in month03, when the world was nearsame metal, and all the grass was unlifeful, and only a few flowers had pushed themselfs up, to be dismembered by the wind.

He was speeding with iced hands and watering eyes when he watched her walking 10m in front of him. It hitted him speedwise that she had changed. They watched each other without a sign, then he turned and followed her, unheartful. He knowed that he was unwatched, nobody would be interested in him. She unspeaked. She walked crosswise thru the grass as tho attempting to leave him.

They goed in the thin unleafed bushs, unuseful for being unwatched or as safeguard from the wind. They stopped. It was ice cold. The windsong thru the tree branchs moved the unfull unclean flowers. He placed his arm round her waist. There was no telescreen, but there were mics, and in the open park, they were able to watch them. But it was unimportant. Nothing was important. If they wanted to sexcrime on the ground, they would be able to, but his skin iced with terror by thinking of it.

She uncountermoved when he holded her; she unattempted to distogether herself. He knowed now what had changed in her. Her face was yellower and a long scar, semi-under her hair, crossed her forehead, but that wasn't the change. Her waist had growed unthinner and, in a shocking way, had hardened. He remembered how he had helped pullout a body from a rocket-bombed house, and had been shocked by the doubleplusoverweigh of the thing, solid and difficult to handle, which maked it nearsame stone.

Her body was nearsame that. He thought that touching her skin would be plusunsame to ante-Miniluv.

He unattempted to kiss her; they unspeaked. As they rewalked thru the grass, she straight-watched him. It was speedful, full of downface and disenjoy. He self-questioned if it was disenjoy from the past, or if it was from the present: his overfull face and watering eyes. They cositted on metal chairs, side-by-side but not overnear. He watched that she was near speaking. She moved her big shoe a few cm and thinkfulwise stepped on an unbig branch. Her foots had growed broader.

'I betrayed you,' Julia speaked, openface.

'I betrayed you,' Smith speaked.

She gived him another speedful face of disenjoy.

'Sometimes, they threaten you with something—something you're unable to withstand, are unable to even think about. And then you speak: "Undo it to me, do it to somebody else, do it to so-and-so." And maybe you act as if, post-questioning, it was only a trick and you untruewise meaned it. But that's untrue. At the time, when it happens, you mean it. You think otherwise to save yourself, and you're plusprepped to save yourself that way. All you care about is yourself.'

'All you care about is yourself,' he respeaked.

'And you feel unsame about the other person.'

'Yes, you feel unsame.'

There was nothing plus to speak about. The wind pushed their thin coveralls to their bodies. Speedwise it becomed shameful to sit there unspeaking. It was overcold to stay, unmoving. She speaked about getting the Tube and upped to go.

'We must remeet,' he speaked.

'Yes, we must remeet.'

He followed her, on-and-off. They unrespeaked. She unattempted to leave him, but walked at a speed so he was unable to stay side-by-side with her. He thinked they would cowalk to the Tube station, but speedwise he was unable to follow in the cold. It was unreasonful. He over-wanted to away from her and return to the Chestnut Tree, which had never been so beautyful as now. He wanted to sit at his corner table, with the newspaper and the gameboard and the ever-streaming harddrink. It was uncold in there. The post-second, not by misstep, he disconnected from her in an unbig crowd of persons. Halfhearted, he attempted to rejoin her, then down-speeded, turned, and walked the opposite way. When he had goed 50m, he backwatched. The street was uncrowded, but he was unable to find her. Any of the speeding persons maybe her. Maybe her unthinned, hardened body was unrecognizable from behind.

'At the time when it happens,' Julia had speaked, 'you mean it.' Smith had meaned it. He hadn't only speaked it, he had wanted it. He had wanted her, and not him, to be...

Something changed in the music that streamed from the telescreen. A breaked and downfaced sound, a yellow sound, comed out of it. And then—maybe it was unhappening, maybe it was only memory—a songer was songing:

'Under the spreading chestnut tree
I dealed you and you dealed me...'

The tears comed to his eyes. A server watched his unfulll glass and returned with the harddrink bottle.

He upped his glass and smelled it. The stuff growed not minus- but plusungood with every mouthful he drinked. But it had become the water he swimmed in. It was his life, his unlife, and his relife. It was harddrink that downed him into unthink every PM, and harddrink that reupped him every AM. When he unsleeped, about 11:00, with red eyes and fireful mouth and unstraight back, it would be unpossible even to unbed if he undrinked a cupful from the bottle placed beside the bed. Thru the AM hours he sitted with blankface, the bottle near, watching the telescreen. From 15:00 to unopening-time, he was at the Chestnut Tree.

Nobody cared what he did, no trumpet unsleeped him, no telescreen loudspeaked at him. Sometimes, maybe 2 times in the workweek, he goed to a dustful, disremembered office in Minitrue and did an unbig workpiece. He had been placed on a subcommittee of a subcommittee which had outgrowed from the unnumbered committees working on minor rewordings of Dictionary number11. They were producing an Interim Report, but what they were reporting on, he never 100% knowed. It was something about the question of if commas should be placed inside brackets, (or outside).

There were 4 others on the doublesubcommittee, all persons nearsame him. There were days when they togethered and then speedwise untogethered, truespeaking to each other that there was nothing to do. But other days they did their workpiece near heartful, making a doubleplusbig show of writing their minutes and long unending memos—when the argument about what they were maybe arguing about growed overcomplex and mazeful, with sharp dealing over words, oversize sidetracks, wars—threats, even, to speak to higher-ups. And then speedwise life would out them, and they would sit round the table watching each other with shadowful eyes, nearsame shadows vaporized by sunlight.

The telescreen stopped speaking. Smith reupped his head. The update! But no, they were only changing the music. He had a mind-map behind his eyelids. The troop-moves was a picture: black arrowing down, and white side- arrowing, thru the tail. As tho wanting help, he upwatched the unworryed face of BB. Was it possible arrow02 unexisted?

His interest redowned. He drinked another mouthful of harddrink, upped the white gamepiece, and maked a maybeful move, but it was the uncorrect move, because...

Uncalled, a memory streamed into his mind. He watched a candlelighted room with plusbig bed and white bedcover, and himself, a youth of age09 or age10, sitting on the floor, playing a game and joyspeaking, excited. His parent was sitting opposite him and also joyspeaking.

She would be vaporized about 1 post-month, but it was a day of retogethering, when the ever-hunger in his belly was disremembered and his luv for her had semi-returned. He plusremembered the day—a raining, over-wet day, when the water downstreamed the window and inside was underlightful for reading books. The 2 youths unenjoyed the unlight, over-unbig bedroom. Smith loudspeaked for feed, moved round the room pulling everything out of place and kicking the walls. The cohabiters banged on the wall, while the youths unjoyspeaked on-and-off. In the end his parent speaked: 'Now, be good, and I'll deal you a game. A beautyful game—you'll luv it.' Then she goed thru the rain, to an unbig market which was on-and-off open, and returned with gameboard and pieces.

He remembered the smell of the wet cardboard. It was doubleplusungood. The board was breaked and the doubleplusunbig wood pieces were malknifed, so they would unfullwise lay on their sides. Smith watched the game, longfaced and uninterested. But then his parent fired a piece of candle, and they sitted on the floor to play. He was animalful excited and loudspeaking with joyspeak as the gamepieces upped and downed. They played 8 games, winning 4 each. His doubleplusunbig sister, overyouthful to understand the game, sitted, joyspeaking because the others were joyspeaking. For a whole day they had all been joyful together.

He pushed the picture out of his mind. It was an untrue memory.

He was worryed by untrue memorys sometimes. They were unimportant, if he recognized them. Somethings had happened, others had unhappened. He returned to the gameboard and reupped the white gamepiece. Nearwise in the same millisecond, it dropped onto the board with a bang. He had jumped as tho an arrow had hitted him. A sharp trumpet-call had ripped the air. It was the newscast! Winners! Ante-newscast trumpet-calls always meaned a win. An electric feeling runned thru the cafe. Even the servers stopped and opened their ears.

The trumpet-call loudspeaked oversize. An excited speaker was on the telescreen, but even as it started it was nearwise overpowered by joyspeaking from outside. The news had flashed round the streets. He was able to hear enough from the telescreen to understand that it had all happened as he had forecasted; a plusbig number of war-boats had, unwatched, speedwise hitted from behind enemy lines, the white arrow ripping thru the tail of the black.

Winful words pushed thru the loudspeak: 'Plusbig planning—100% correct coworking—100% win—500,000 POWs —100% dishearten the enemy—control the world—bring the war near-end—winners—doubleplusbiggest win in history—win, win, win!'

Under-table, Smith's foots maked uncontrolled moves. He had unmoved from his chair, but in his mind he was running, running, he was with the crowds outside, over-joyspeaking. He reupwatched the BB picture. The over-man of the world! The stonewall which safeguarded Oceania! 10 ante-minutes—yes, only 10 ante-minutes—he had been untrueheartful, as he thinked if the frontline news was win or unwin. He had pluschanged in Miniluv, but the final, ever-needed, rewholeful change had unhappened until now.

The telescreen was outstreaming the news story of POWs and money and killing, but the loudspeaking outside had downed. The servers were returning to their work. They bringed the harddrink bottle. Smith, sitting in a joyful dream, was unattentionful as his glass was fulled up. He was unrunning, unjoyspeaking. He was in Miniluv, everything was OK, his mind was white as paper.

He upwatched the oversize face. It had taked him 40 years to learn what joyface was under the black mustache. Coldhearted, unneeded misunderstanding! Unmoved, headstrong outsider from luv! Harddrink-scented tears downstreamed the sides of his nose. But it was OK, everything was OK, the mind-war had ended. He was winful over himself.

He luved BB.